'Housekeepers come and go, but a wife stays.'

Thus Philippe, the émigré Comte de Sevignac, instructs his man, Junot, to find him a housekeeper wife. For alone, he can no longer battle to restore his family fortune lost in the French Revolution.

Lucy Forster, young, widowed and practically destitute is willing to accept almost any position and, thanks to the Count's wily French servant, soon finds herself agreeing to marry Philippe.

Being mistress of the delapidated Brooktye Farm and its thriving new vineyards is a daunting prospect, yet Lucy comes to love the house—and its master. But how can she ever hope to win his love when all his attention is centred on the grape harvest rather than on his beautiful new wife?

Marriage of Strangers

Elizabeth Hart

MILLS & BOON LIMITED
London · Sydney · Toronto

First published in Great Britain 1982
by Mills & Boon Limited, 15–16 Brook's Mews,
London W1A 1DR

ISBN 0 263 74112 5

04/0183

Set in 10 on 11 pt Linotron Times

Photoset by Rowland Phototypesetting Ltd
Bury St Edmunds, Suffolk
Made and printed in Great Britain by
Cox & Wyman Ltd, Reading

CHAPTER ONE

'No, I fear you would not suit this position, Mrs Forster. You are not at all what I had in mind.'

Lucy Forster stared at the cold, imperious woman confronting her, too shocked to feel anything but bewilderment. 'I am afraid I don't understand, Lady Stansgate.'

'Quite frankly, Mrs Forster, when Mr Haverfield told me he knew of a widow who would be able to instruct my daughters in all the necessary accomplishments, I had pictured someone more mature. And, to be honest, a little less—worldly than yourself.' Lady Stansgate contemplated the slim figure before her, the mass of coppery hair crowned by a brown bonnet and the pale face from which gazed a pair of blue-green eyes. 'I cannot imagine you would find the sober, rural life we lead here at Stansgate Park at all to your taste.'

So, thought Lucy, it had after all been a mistake to wear Kitty's cast-off travelling gown! Despite being at least three years out-of-date and therefore no longer acceptable to her stepmother, it gave her a deceptive air of stylishness. Yet, if Lady Stansgate did but realise, she had virtually no choice. Drawing in a deep breath and controlling her steadily rising anger, she said evenly, 'My age is twenty-four and I have been a widow for over six years. For most of that time I have been obliged to live in London with my father and stepmother, but my childhood was spent near the Kentish Downs. It is now my dearest wish to return to the country, as Mr

Haverfield is aware. That is why he recommended me for this post.'

It had been agreed when Mr Haverfield, her father's lawyer, first offered to help her find a position as governess that they would not reveal how desperate was her situation unless it became absolutely necessary. Unconsciously Lucy's hands clenched in her lap. She *must* secure this post! To find another might take time and she had very little money left to live on—enough for a few days and no more. Yet Lady Stansgate's proud, unsympathetic stare made her more determined than ever not to plead poverty.

'You were widowed very young, Mrs Forster.' Lady Stansgate's tone was sceptical. 'I find it surprising you have not married again. Surely you have not lacked the opportunity?'

Lucy flushed. 'I fail to see this has anything to do with the situation, Lady Stansgate. The fact is I am a widow who is prepared to live in the country—and you require someone to instruct your daughters. May I inquire their ages?'

Lady Stansgate stiffened. 'Ambrosine is twelve and Seraphina ten. I also have a son, Ninian, who is fourteen—but naturally he has his own tutor.' Her voice softened noticeably on mentioning her son, then at once grew hard again. 'However, there is little point in our continuing this conversation since I have already made my decision. I trust you will be able to catch the evening stage from Cuckfield back to London?'

Lucy turned pale and tried to control her trembling hands. Lifting her chin she declared, 'I am not satisfied, Lady Stansgate. Have the goodness to inform me why I am not suitable.'

Lady Stansgate stared at her in disbelief. She was a tall woman, willowy rather than statuesque, with fair, almost white hair and sharply modelled features. Her eyes were undoubtedly her best asset, wide-spaced and a clear unclouded blue, but it was difficult to imagine them ever being filled with warmth or affection for anyone, save possibly her son. At this moment they were cold as sapphires. 'I was under the impression I had already done so.'

'No,' said Lucy in a reasonable tone. 'You have expressed doubts that I should be contented living in the country and I have assured you such doubts are unfounded, since I am well used to such a life. As far as I can discover you have no other objections.'

'You are too young!' snapped Lady Stansgate.

'Not all that young, surely. And in my experience young people often respond more readily to someone not too far removed in age from themselves.'

'And you are impertinent! As I thought, you have neither the temperament nor the experience to be a governess. A governess, indeed! No, Mrs Forster, as I knew from the moment you walked into this room, you are not suited to this position and I cannot imagine what possessed Mr Haverfield to send you to me. I will instruct one of the grooms to return you to Cuckfield in the gig. Kindly wait here until you are sent for.' Giving Lucy no chance to protest at this summary dismissal, she swept from the room.

Left alone, Lucy's defiance ebbed swiftly away. By her stubborn pride she had ruined her chances of a secure future. What hope was there for her now— homeless, penniless, her father behind the bars of a debtors' prison and her stepmother Kitty taking refuge with her young son in the bosom of her own family? Lucy sighed. It was undoubtedly Kitty's fault that Charles Tennant had sold his estate in Kent, along with his hunters, his greyhounds and all the trappings of a country squire, in order to provide her with the life in London she craved; yet he had always been a gambler ever since

Lucy could remember. His wife's extravagances had merely served as an excuse for him to return to the tables again and again, finally losing every penny he had.

How their lives had changed since that fateful year of 1799! She herself had been wed and widowed within the space of a few short months; her father had recovered from a near-fatal fever and gone to recuperate in Bath, whence he had returned with a young bride. Kitty, soon bored with country pastimes, had insisted they remove themselves to more civilised surroundings almost at once. Lucy herself had been too numbed with grief by the news of her husband's death fighting with General Abercrombie in the Low Countries to take in fully the significance of this new upheaval; but she had had ample time since then to appreciate the devastating manner in which it had changed their lives.

I once thought one could stoop no lower than to seek employment as a governess, she reflected; *now it seems the most desirable and yet unattainable aim in life!*

The lackey who came to inform her that the gig was waiting regarded her with open curiosity. As Lucy followed him along a passageway she caught a glimpse of imposing panelled hall and carved oaken staircase upon which stood a man, heavily built and of above average height, with a floridly handsome countenance, who was actually leaning forward so that he might have a better view of her. For a second their eyes met. His were a strange yellow-green and narrowed speculatively as they swept over her figure. Suddenly Lucy became aware that Kitty's cast-off gown was a shade too small for her. Though they were about the same height her stepmother was a slight, ethereal creature, restless as a butterfly. On Lucy the bronze velvet redingote fitted a little too snugly, outlining her breasts and the curve of her hips—a fact that was certainly not lost upon the man now staring at her with frank admiration.

Lucy flushed and turned immediately to follow her guide. Could that objectionable person have been Sir Ralph Stansgate? she wondered. If so, he might easily be the real reason why Lady Stansgate had decided not to offer her employment, for by the look of him he was undoubtedly a man with an eye for a good female figure. It was perhaps a more understandable reason—at any rate a more flattering one—for the failure of her journey. Nonetheless it did not alter the fact that she was now on her way back to London, and as she climbed into the gig her spirits sank to the bottom of her well-worn boots.

It was not the same coachman who had met her with the carriage at Cuckfield and who had been handsomely attired in livery. How her heart had lifted when she was transported through the great iron gates into Stansgate Park and along the drive lined with graceful beeches! This had been William's country. Only a few miles from here he had been born, gone to school, helped his father on the farm until finally running away to join the militia. So little she had known of him, her beloved young husband; coming to Sussex had seemed a golden opportunity to revive what few memories she had.

Now she found herself sitting beside a fresh-complexioned, grey-haired old groom, who reminded her of the Kentish countrymen she had known as a child. As they bowled along behind the chestnut mare she began chatting to him and learned he had worked on the Stansgate estate all his life. 'Born in one of the cottages over there, t'other side of wood,' he told her in his soft Sussex accent.

'Is the estate very extensive?' she inquired, preferring to make conversation rather than let her mind dwell upon her predicament.

'Large enough. He were an empire-builder, old Sir Ninian!' The old man shook his head and gave a reminiscent chuckle. 'Bought up every farm around here that fell under the hammer.'

'Is Ninian a family name? I believe Lady Stansgate told me her son was called Ninian.'

'Aye, that's it. He's no chip off the old block, though! Little scrawny fellow—can't hardly get him up on a horse! Old Sir Ninian used to have the finest seat in the County. See that white house over there?' He waved his whip in the direction of a building half hidden among massive oaks. 'That's the Dower House, where his widow lives. Lady Emilie. She's a termagant!' He wheezed appreciatively.

Lucy looked in the direction he had indicated and remarked, 'There's a carriage driving out of the gates and coming towards us. Would that be—?'

'Oh, aye—that's her. On her way up to the Park to make sure everything's running smoothly. She don't trust her grandson further'n she can see him!'

Thinking that Sir Ralph, if it were indeed he she had seen on the stairs, looked as though he were in his late thirties at least, she observed, 'Lady Emilie must be a great age.'

'Nigh on eighty,' agreed the old man, touching his forelock as the carriage drew near. It was an open landau, driven by a liveried coachman and containing two ladies, one of whom was plainly an insignificant companion. The other, impressively gowned in purple silk trimmed with black braid, was an elderly lady with hair white as snow and highly-rouged cheeks. She acknowledged the old man's salute and raised her eyeglass to stare at Lucy as they passed—no doubt also assessing her unsuitability as a governess, Lucy thought with a sigh, and even now on her way to applaud her grand-daughter-in-law's decision.

The groom deposited her in the courtyard of 'The Talbot' inn at Cuckfield, courteously wishing her a good journey back to London. Lucy bade him goodbye and turned sadly into the inn. To her relief it was not too crowded. 'When do you expect the next coach to London?' she asked the landlord.

'Within the hour,' he answered, adding doubtfully, 'But odds are you won't find a seat on it, ma'am. The Prince himself is at Brighthelmstone this week and there's a deal of coming and going. Most of the coaches are full when they reach Cuckfield. You might find a seat on the Mail . . .'

'At what time would that be?'

'About twenty minutes past midnight.'

She stared at him. 'Past *midnight*—!'

'I fear so, ma'am. It arrives at Blossoms Inn in Cheapside at six o'clock tomorrow morning.'

'Six o'clock!' she echoed again, trying not to show her dismay. The thought of travelling all night on a Mail coach to arrive in the City at dawn, weary and travel-stained and with nowhere to go, was daunting in the extreme.

The landlord regarded her with concern. 'Perhaps you might like to fill in the time with some refreshment, ma'am. You look a bit on the weary side, if I may say so. There's a small private table over here, just suitable for a lady . . .'

Lucy smiled at him gratefully and realised she was indeed feeling tired, chilly and extremely empty. Trying to recall exactly how much she had in her purse, she said hesitantly, 'Thank you, landlord. Perhaps a bowl of soup—?'

'I can recommend the veal, ma'am.'

'No, thank you. I am not very hungry. A bowl of soup will do well enough.' She tried to make her tone convincing.

The soup was brought by the landlord's wife, a round bustling soul with cheeks flushed from stooping over a hot stove. 'This should warm you, m'dear. Still gets nippy of an evening, don't it?'

'It does indeed,' Lucy agreed.

The soup was too hot to be supped immediately, although in truth she was so ravenous she could have disposed of it all in five minutes even at the risk of scalding her throat. But there were hours yet before the arrival of the Mail, and somehow she must contrive to pass the time without spending any more money.

When she had finished eating she rested her head against the back of the seat, soon drifting off into a light, fitful sleep.

Some time later she awoke with a start and sat bolt upright, wondering if she had slept too long, but a glance at the clock told her it was still only half-past nine. The taproom was empty apart from two labourers playing cribbage in a far corner, and there was no sound from the street outside. Indeed, the only signs of life seemed to be coming from a closed door behind her, a murmur of conversation punctuated by shouts of good-humoured laughter. The landlord and his wife must be entertaining privately, she decided, and by the tantalising smells drifting past her nose they were also enjoying a substantial meal.

She sighed and stretched her cramped limbs. The effect of the soup had worn off all too quickly. Once more she was aware of a gnawing hunger which made it difficult to concentrate on the urgent matter of deciding what she should do when she returned to London.

During the course of the six years spent in the tall house in Wimpole Street she had made few real friends. The people who called were either gambling cronies of her father's or Kitty's admirers, and she had little in common with any of them. Her position as a widowed daughter with a stepmama only a few years older than herself was a difficult one and as their financial situation grew more and mor precarious she hardly mixed in company at all. No, there was no-one in London to whom she could turn for help.

A single tear of self-pity rolled down her cheek. Despising her weakness she brushed it away and tried to focus her mind on a solution. If only she need not return to London at all! If only she could find some other employment here in Sussex, so that she might stay in the countryside of which William had been so fond. Almost anything would do, and surely there must be some family in need of a reliable, trustworthy servant. This was a county sandwiched between London and the newly-fashionable Brighthelmstone on the coast, inhabited largely by well-to-do families who liked to be within reach of both; families less grand, perhaps, than the Stansgates of Stansgate Park, but then social standing was not her prime concern. Perhaps the landlord might know of just such a family . . .

Full of resolution she rose to her feet, intending to knock upon the door of the kitchen whence issued such cheerful sounds, but no sooner had she taken a few steps than a wave of faintness swept over her and she fell unconscious to the ground.

When she regained her senses she found herself lying on a sofa, regarded by three anxious faces. 'There,' m'dear, what a fright you gave us, to be sure! Such a bang as you went down, but it was not your head, praise be to God, only your arm. I fear you'll have a tidy bruise there before long.' The landlord's wife patted her sympathetically. 'A drop of brandy, if you please, Tom.'

Lucy struggled to sit up and accepted the glass of brandy the landlord held out to her. He watched her for a moment and then turned to his wife. ''Tis my belief,

Mrs Best, that what the young lady needs is food—and plenty of it!'

'No, please!' Lucy protested. 'There's no need . . .'

'We have some to spare.' A plateful of steaming roast veal and vegetables was placed on the table. 'Do you feel well enough to move a little nearer?'

'Yes, but I'm putting you to so much trouble.' Lucy looked anxiously round and saw that the third member of the party was a small man of indeterminate age with a shiny, rubicund face and sandy hair hanging in wisps from a high-domed forehead. 'And I'm disturbing you when you have company . . .'

'Oh, Lor'—that's only Junot!' exclaimed Mrs Best, smiling genially. 'He often drops in of a Wednesday evening.' She gave a chuckle. 'He's a Froggie from across the water. But not a spy, I promise you!'

'I am plissed to meet you, Madame,' said Junot, with a pronounced accent.

'Came over with one of the émigré families during the Terror,' added the landlord. 'Was it ten years ago now, Junot?'

'Twelve,' corrected Junot, grinning widely.

'Twelve, was it? Don't time fly!' Mrs Best gave the little Frenchman an affectionate tap on the shoulder and then turned to see how Lucy was progressing. 'Come on, m'dear—eat up! You'll feel a deal better with something inside you.'

Obediently Lucy ate, and soon began to feel much better. The colour returned to her cheeks and Mrs Best looked at her with approval. 'What a foolish thing to do,' she said softly. 'No sense in going without food, you know.'

Lucy flushed. 'My mind was full of other things,' she said lamely. 'I suppose I just—forgot.'

They all three regarded her with such sympathetic understanding that she found herself confiding in them.

She was careful to avoid mentioning the Stansgate family by name, though it must have been obvious to them
who her prospective employers had been. 'But having
come to Sussex,' she concluded, 'I am reluctant to leave
it again. I really don't mind what I do to earn my keep,
but I must find something quickly, for—as you rightly
guessed—I have little left in the way of funds. I suppose
it would be too much to hope that you might know of
something . . . ?'

Mr Best scratched his head. 'There's nothing springs
to mind straight away. I mean, there's some things just
ain't suitable. I can't imagine a lady like you taking a
position as housemaid, for example . . .'

Mrs Best drew in her breath sharply and gave him a
quelling look, but Lucy said earnestly, 'I cannot afford
to be too proud, Mr Best. My situation is somewhat
desperate. I will consider anything.'

Mrs Best tutted to herself and rocked back and forth
in her chair. 'Widowed so young,' she murmured. 'Such
a tragedy, dying for his country . . . And a young man
from around these parts, you say?'

Lucy nodded and stared down at her hands, unwilling
to let her thoughts dwell on William. 'All that is in the
past,' she murmured. 'I must think now of the future.'
But the future looked so bleak that once again she felt a
betraying tear escape.

'Hey, hey!' exclaimed the Frenchman, quick to per-
ceive her emotion. He gestured frantically to the landlord. 'A glass for Madame! We will bring a leetle sun-
shine into her life, *non*?'

A glass was set in front of her and filled with sparkling
golden wine. Lucy wiped her eyes and asked incredulously, 'My goodness—is that champagne?'

'As near as makes no difference,' Mrs Best proclaimed. 'Taste it, m'dear, and see what you think.'

Lucy sipped at the wine and found it lighter than

champagne but decidedly pleasing to the palate. 'I like it very much indeed,' she told them, 'but I thought such luxuries were denied us while the War lasts?'

At this they burst out laughing and Junot shook all over as if it were a huge joke. Mystified, Lucy wondered if the wine had been smuggled over from France, possibly by Junot himself, which would explain why he was so pleased by her approval, but she decided it was wiser not to inquire too closely. She smiled at the Frenchman and said, 'I only hope it won't befuddle my wits. I must keep a clear head if I'm to find a solution to my problems before the Mail coach arrives.'

Junot cleared his throat and said abruptly, '*We* could offer you a position. My master—he needs someone . . .'

They all stared at him. 'That Mollie Thrupp,' said Mrs Best, pursing her lips, 'is a slattern.' She turned to Lucy. 'And as for the state of that kitchen—'

'That is so,' Junot agreed quickly. 'But we need someone else—for the house.' He looked a little uncomfortable and for the first time his smile had disappeared, to be replaced by a slight frown.

'Where does your master live?' Lucy inquired.

'' 'Tis a farm not far from here,' said Mrs Best. 'The real name is Brooktye, but everyone calls it Frenchman's on account of Mr de Sevignac being a Frenchman, you see . . .' Her voice died away as she looked doubtfully at Junot.

'Ah, yes—the émigré,' said Lucy, enlightened. 'But what would the position be, exactly?' From Junot's expression she strongly suspected there might be no such position and he had spoken impulsively out of a desire to help her.

In confirmation of her suspicions he shifted uneasily on his chair and looked at the landlord and his wife. 'I will explain to Madame . . .' He then said nothing further but only stared meaningly at them.

There was an awkward pause before Mrs Best sprang to her feet. 'Of course! Come along, Tom. You and I have work to do.' She took her bemused spouse by the arm and led him from the room.

Left alone with Lucy, Junot still looked ill-at-ease and seemed unable to begin, so she prompted him encouragingly. 'This position . . . ?'

'Ah, yes,' he said. 'The position. Your papa is—how d'you call it—a yeoman?'

'A yeoman?' She was puzzled. 'I am used to living on a farm, if that is what concerns you.'

'That is good.' Junot nodded.

'Is it a housekeeper that your master requires?'

'No, not a housekeeper. What he tells me is—Junot, he says, you find me a whiff.'

'A whiff?' she repeated, uncomprehending.

'Yes, a whiff. Housekeepers, they come and go. Whiffs must stay. What we need, he says, is someone who will see to our comfort. Not a grand lady but a simple woman of good yeoman stock.' He grinned, with returning confidence. 'And now that Madame is dead he is free to marry again! So—we look for a whiff.'

She stared at him. 'You surely cannot mean—a *wife*?'

He nodded vigorously. 'Yes—a whiff! Is much better than a housekeeper. You would have good position, best in the County.' Visibly he swelled with pride. 'My master is a nobleman. In France he was heir to a grand chateau, but in '93 he was forced to flee the country with his papa and his whiff and come to England.' His face grew mournful. 'But, alas, the papa dies. It is too much for him, you understand, to leave his home and make a new life in a strange country. And now, the whiff too is dead!' His smile miraculously reappeared and spread wider than ever. 'So Monsieur may take a new whiff. *You*, Madame!'

'I don't think so.' Lucy could not help being amused by Junot's calm assumption that wives were so easy to come by. 'After all, I've never even met your master—'

Junot lifted his shoulders and flung his hands wide in a gesture of bewilderment. 'But what does that signify? In France such marriages are arranged. *Eh bien*, now I am arranging it!' He looked pleased with himself. 'You will suit my master very well, I think. It will be a good match.'

Smiling, Lucy shook her head. 'I'm afraid not, Junot. In England ladies are not in the habit of marrying gentlemen they have never met. But if you *are* in need of a housekeeper—'

'Why you not want to be a whiff?' Junot demanded. 'You are a widow and you are young. You *should* marry again!'

'Perhaps I shall, one day,' she replied. 'But at the moment it is not my intention. What I require is not a husband but a position—and if you and your master really do need a housekeeper then perhaps we could come to some arrangement. Would it be possible for me to visit the farm?'

'But yes!' He grinned broadly. 'Tomorrow I come and take you to my master.'

'Will you, Junot?' Lucy began to feel hopeful for the first time since her interview with Lady Stansgate. She added cautiously, 'But you must make it clear to your master than I am applying for the post of housekeeper—and nothing else!'

Junot nodded and beamed happily.

CHAPTER
TWO

A LITTLE after midnight the Mail coach rumbled through the empty streets of Cuckfield, made a brief stop and then departed again, leaving the town to sink back into its silent slumbers. Lucy, in an upstairs room at the Talbot, where Mrs Best had insisted she spend the night as their guest, heard it and turned over in bed. Now that it had gone she could sleep. She had made her bid for independence, and whatever the morrow might bring she could not be sorry that the coach was continuing on its way without her.

She slept surprisingly well, considering all the uncertainties surrounding her, and in the morning made ready to be collected by Junot. It would have to be the bronze redingote again: she had nothing else with her at all appropriate for an interview. Surveying her reflection in the inadequate looking-glass she felt far from confident she would make the right impression upon a prospective employer. Despairingly she pushed her bright, rebellious curls out of sight beneath her bonnet and composed her face in what she hoped was a proper matronly expression.

When Mrs Best appeared with the news that Junot was waiting below Lucy drew a deep breath and said, 'Oh, dear, I do hope I can persuade this Frenchman that I would make him a suitable housekeeper. Otherwise—'

Mrs Best sat down suddenly on the edge of the bed and declared, 'It will not do. I cannot let you go?'

Lucy stared at her. 'Whatever do you mean?'

'What I say. A young lady like you, going to live at Brooktye—it wouldn't be right.'

'Why not? What is he like—this Frenchman?' It would be hypocritical to pretend she was not curious, especially in view of Junot's outrageous proposition the previous evening.

'Oh, a well-enough *looking* gentleman. But odd.'

'In what way—odd?'

'Keeps himself to himself, you might say. Don't mix with the local folk at all, not like Junot. A strange man and a bitter one.' Mrs Best regarded Lucy with troubled eyes. 'Not surprising, I suppose, when you consider how the Revolution has robbed him of his inheritance. Though there's some that say he has a tidy pile hidden away somewhere!'

'If that is the case, why should he become a farmer?'

'Farmer!' Mrs Best heaved her substantial shoulders in a sceptical shrug. 'An odd sort of farming goes on up there, I can tell you.'

'Well, Junot seems to have remained loyal to him, if he came over with the family during the Terror and has stayed with him ever since.'

'Ah, Junot!' Mrs Best smiled fondly. 'He is a rare one, our Junot. You can trust him. He will see that you come to no harm.'

'Then you may let me go with a clear conscience. All I want to do is look at the house. If there is the slightest doubt in my mind I shall not take the position, I promise you.' Lucy fixed her with an earnest look.

'Very well. But while you are there I shall rack my brains for some alternative,' said Mrs Best obstinately. 'By the time you return I shall have thought of something, depend upon it.'

Half-an-hour later Lucy sat beside Junot in an antiquated phaeton drawn by a heavy black mare. They plodded ponderously along the road towards Staplefield, giving Lucy ample time to admire the fine vew to the south of the Downs, crowned by the dark mass of trees that formed Chanctonbury Ring. It was a bright May morning and there was an air of expectancy about the countryside, the hedgerows in bud and the fields full of young life. Lucy turned to Junot and remarked impulsively, 'This is my kind of countryside! I feel at home here. Do you ever long, Junot, for your native land?'

He sighed deeply. '*La France*—' he kissed his fingers—'is a beautiful woman and I love her very much. It break my heart to leave her but, alas, at the moment she is being unfaithful so one must turn elsewhere. England, she is not so beautiful, perhaps, but she is kind. Yes, England is a fair mistress—a very fair mistress indeed.'

Lucy laughed. 'But is she really kind, I wonder? Have you always found a welcome here?'

'Ah!' He gave an eloquent shrug. 'Not always, perhaps. When I first arrive, with the old Comte de Sevignac, we stay near Brighthelmstone until all aliens are ordered to move away from the coast because of the threat of invasion. So we come inland, to live with Monsieur le Comte's relations by marriage. There is not so easy, especially for me.' A rueful smile spread over his face. 'The housemaids are all afraid of me, because I am French. They expect to be murdered in their beds—or worse!'

'Where did you come from, in France?'

'From the Haute Marne, near Epernay. But the old Comte spent much of his time at Court. Alas, he was one of those accused of plotting to help the King escape from the Temple, so it become necessary for us to leave France *toute suite*. We take a few belongings and flee to England. Hey, hey!' A sigh of melancholy escaped him, to be swiftly replaced by determined cheerfulness. 'But it is better to be poor and alive than rich and dead, as my master so often says.'

'When did the old Comte die, Junot?'

'A few months after we arrive. He is already a sick man and has not the will to make a fresh start in a new country.'

'So now his son is the Comte de Sevignac?'

He nodded. 'But in England he is a plain mister. Mr de Sevignac, that is how he wish to be called. Except that in Sussex they cannot say the name at all, so instead they call him "the Frenchman".'

'And Madame de Sevignac—how did she die? She must have been very young . . .'

Junot dismissed the lady with a short laugh. 'Ah, she! Milady could not abide the English weather. After a year she returns to France and now we hear she has perished of a fever . . .'

'But how dreadful for your master!'

Junot looked surprised. 'He did not mind. He never cared much for her anyway.'

'Then why—?' Lucy checked herself. 'Oh, I suppose it was another of your arranged marriages.'

He made no answer but stirred the mare's lazy rump with the tip of his whip. Giving him a sidelong glance Lucy saw he was wearing a complacent smile and for a moment was tempted to reiterate her concern that she should be presented to M de Sevignac as a prospective housekeeper and nothing more; but she decided against doing so on the grounds that the matter would be soonest forgotten if it were not resurrected. Instead she turned her gaze outwards to dwell on the pleasing sight of rich farmland graced by oak and ash, elm and beech, many of the trees a considerable age, bearing witness to the time long ago when this wealden countryside was so thickly forested that the South Saxons living on the coast were effectively cut off from the rest of England.

Without any apparent signal from Junot the mare turned left down a narrow track and Lucy saw in front of her a farmhouse of great charm, constructed in brick and tile with a much-weathered roof and substantial chimney-stacks betraying its Tudor origin. 'Is that Brooktye? But it is beautiful!' she exclaimed.

'It is well enough,' agreed Junot, adding enigmatically, 'At least it has one good field that faces south . . .'

She did not inquire into the significance of this remark, for already she was distracted by the realisation that the beauty of Brooktye diminished as they drew nearer, marred by the unmistakable signs of decay and neglect. What had once been a well laid out garden in front of the house was now choked with weeds, dilapidated outbuildings stood empty and chickens ran across the yard in front of them, pecking for corn amidst a dirty mess of old hay and horse dung that looked as though it had not been cleared for months. Lucy's spirits began to sink, but she took a resolute hold of them, warning herself against over-hasty judgments.

Her first sight of the interior of Brooktye did little to reassure her. Junot led her straight into the kitchen, a long low room dominated by a black-leaded range and a great oak table capable of seating twenty farm-hands at harvest-time with ease. This was plainly the oldest part of the house and the dark beams supporting the ceiling were in themselves attractive, but sadly the copper pots and pans hung upon them were in dire need of a good clean. The fine wood of the table was dull and smeared with bacon grease and the range bore visible signs of most of the meals cooked upon it in the last few months, if not years. As she walked across the floor she heard something crunch beneath her feet and, glancing down, saw that the red flagstones were covered by a carpet of crumbs and bits of straw brought in from the yard. A breeding ground for mice and even rats, she thought;

and the one-eyed cat curled up on the range looked too
lethargic to bother with keeping down the vermin.

Seated in a rush chair beside the range was a woman
who started to her feet when they entered and rubbed
her eyes dazedly as though they had just awoken her
from a deep sleep. Lucy stared at her curiously, remembering Mrs Best's description of Mollie Thrupp as a
slattern. Certainly she looked none too clean but she was
younger than Lucy had imagined and good-looking in a
bold, gypsy fashion. Dark-eyed and olive-skinned, with
high cheekbones and a wide, full-lipped mouth, she had
a careless animal grace. Strands of coarse black hair
hung down from beneath her cap and the bodice of her
torn and food-stained dress was stretched taut across a
generous bosom. She returned Lucy's stare with a sullen
look.

'Wait here,' Junot instructed. 'I will fetch my master.'

Left alone with Mrs Thrupp Lucy could think of
nothing to say. She had no desire to sit on any of the
chairs and such idle pleasantries as commenting upon
the house seemed inappropriate, so she remained standing in the centre of the room, all too aware that Mollie
Thrupp was regarding her with some hostility.

At last the woman spoke. 'Did he send for you—the
Frenchman?'

Lucy bit her lip, reluctant to divulge the true reason
for her presence. If no-one had informed Mollie Thrupp
that her employer was seeking a housekeeper then the
woman's resentment was understandable.

'Hoity-toity,' muttered Mollie under her breath, mis-
interpreting her silence. 'Well, you won't suit here, and
that's the truth! I can take care of all his Lordship's needs
well enough . . .' She gave a low laugh and thrust her
face close to Lucy's. 'He don't care for fine ladies no
more, so you're wasting your time.'

Instinctively Lucy drew back, revolted by the strong

smell of drink on Mollie Thrupp's breath. Fortunately at that moment Junot returned, beaming broadly. 'He is coming! Monsieur is coming . . .'

Lucy was disconcerted. She had expect to be conducted to a more congenial room for her interview. Was she really to be questioned here in the kitchen, with Mrs Thrupp as interested spectator?

But Junot was already shooing the woman from the room. 'Go and feed the hens,' he urged her impatiently.

'It's cold out in that yard!' protested Mollie.

'Then go somewhere else!' Placing both hands on her rounded posterior he literally pushed her down three steps and along a dark passage. A door slammed shut and he came back, dusting his hands.

'So that,' remarked Lucy, raising an eyebrow, 'is Mollie Thrupp?'

He said apologetically, 'It is not easy to find someone who will work here. Because we are French, you understand?'

'I understand.'

'It is not right that my master lives in this way . . .' Junot demonstrated by his gesture that he was not insensible to the squalor surrounding him, and then his gaze went past Lucy to the door behind her. 'Monsieur!'

Lucy turned quickly to confront M. de Sevignac. She was perhaps already prepared not to expect the typical French aristocrat she had encountered in London; nonetheless she was shocked to find herself looking at a man as casually dressed as a labourer, in the act of rolling down his shirtsleeves. His boots were mud-spattered and so were his breeches, but his dark hair was tousled and damp as if he had just plunged his head hastily beneath the tap. Against the whiteness of his shirt his skin looked very brown and he was tall—tall enough to have to bow his head low as he entered the kitchen to

avoid the beams. Deep lines seamed his face on either
side of his mouth, giving him a world-weary, ravaged
look. He returned Lucy's stare in silence, his grey eyes
resting upon her seemingly with indifference.

Junot plunged forward and eagerly made the necessary introductions, resorting almost at once to his native
tongue. Fortunately Lucy had learned the language
from a native Frenchwoman who was at one time her
governess, so she was able to follow their conversation
with ease; and what she heard gave her cause for consternation.

'Is she not exactly as I described?' Junot began. 'What
more could you ask—?'

'Of good yeoman stock, I said. She looks too fine to
me.'

'Her father was a farmer. She has spent all her life in
the country. And she is desperate! She has nowhere else
to go—'

'Why is she desperate? Have you asked yourself,
Junot, if she is completely honest? Her father is in gaol,
you tell me. Would you have me marry a felon's daughter?'

'You have only to look at her to know that she is
honest!'

'Where women are concerned, my friend, you are
notoriously lacking in judgment. I have already made
one mistake. I have no wish to make another.'

'Monsieur! Ask yourself—where shall we find a better
wife? One who is accustomed to life in the country, yet
who has the gracious manners of a lady? One who is a
widow, moreover, and therefore—'

'She looks too young to be a widow.'

'Her husband was killed in the war—she told me so.
And she is beautiful—'

'Her looks are of secondary importance to me. Will
she *work*?—that's what matters. And will she stay, or go

running back to London as soon as she tires of this life we lead?'

'If you marry her, she *must* stay!'

Unable to bear this a second longer, Lucy resolved to speak, though deciding it would be prudent not to reveal her knowledge of the French language. 'Monsieur,' she began, 'I should be grateful if you would outline exactly what my duties would be, as *housekeeper*. Also, I should like to see the rest of the house . . .'

He stared at her uncomprehendingly and turned again to Junot. 'What is she talking about?'

'I told her we need someone to run the house,' Junot explained, 'and she mistook my meaning.'

'But she is not at all the sort of woman one would employ as a housekeeper . . .'

'Exactly!'

Perhaps he spoke no English at all, thought Lucy. In desperation she appealed to Junot. 'Is there some problem? Perhaps your master has decided I would not be suitable for the post . . . ?'

'It is not a question of suitability, Madame,' interposed M. de Sevignac in English as perfect as her own, with only the faintest trace of accent. 'It is merely that Junot has been a little precipitate, since the idea of engaging a housekeeper had not entered my head.'

She looked reproachfully at Junot, who responded with a helpless shrug. Turning back to his master she said, with all the calm she could muster, 'In that case, Monsieur, I had better leave. I am sorry to have wasted your time . . .' Pretending an unconcern she certainly did not feel she took a few steps towards the door.

'Now, Madame, it is *you* who is being precipitate!'

Arrested by his tone she stopped to look at him in surprise and saw he was frowning deeply, an expression which did little to lighten the formidable lines of his dark countenance.

'Come with me,' he said abruptly, turning on his heel.

She followed him through a panelled hall of fine proportions but with the same neglected, dust-coated air as the kitchen, into a room so sumptuously furnished it took her breath away.

'But this is amazing!' she exclaimed. 'And very French . . .'

'It is the only room in the house furnished by my wife. I fear it is far too ornate for my taste. I never use it.'

'I see,' said Lucy, at a loss for words. The room smelled musty and damp, and on the walls were hung portraits so encrusted with grime it was impossible to tell whether their subjects were male or female. M. de Sevignac moved to the window and pulled back the half-drawn green velvet drapes, disturbing a cloud of dust. Immediately the sunlight streamed in, revealing festoons of cobwebs hanging from the ceiling.

He glanced up at them and frowned. 'You must realise I've had little time in recent years to bother about the niceties of life. From early morning until dusk I work out-of-doors, and when I finish I am too tired to care about my surroundings.'

Lucy looked at him with sympathy. Now that she saw him in a good light she could appreciate how fine-drawn were his features and how weary his grey eyes, yet for all his haggard appearance and the casual manner of his dress he had still that unmistakable air of superiority which had done little to endear the French nobility to the common populace. What a total reversal of his fortunes it must be to find himself here in England, deprived of his lands and forced to wrest a living from the soil . . .

'Pray don't waste your sympathy on me!' he said sharply, rightly interpreting her expression.

Lucy flushed. 'I'm sorry. I—'

'You see before you a fortunate man,' he went on, an almost fanatical gleam in his eye. 'A man with a purpose in life. Come here.' He beckoned her to join him at the window. 'I will show you something I'll wager you've never seen in your life before.'

Nervously she went to stand beside him, her gaze following his pointing finger. She saw before her a garden with cherubic statues, chipped and covered in bird-lime, standing forlornly by a stagnant pond. However it was not the garden he was indicating but the land beyond, which was given over to some kind of fruit ranged in neat rows, presenting a sharp contrast to the disorder evident elsewhere at Brooktye. Aware that he was awaiting her comment she venture, 'It reminds me of the hop-fields in my native Kent, yet I do not think—'

'Vines!' he said triumphantly. 'You are looking at what I believe may be the only working vineyard in England. And this October, God willing, should see another good harvest . . .'

'A vineyard!' breathed Lucy, staring at the scene before her. 'But I would not have thought such a thing possible in our English climate—'

'Ah, now that is where you are mistaken.' His eyes were glowing with enthusiasm, making him look at least ten years younger. 'For centuries every English monastery had its vineyard and produced its own wine. It was your misguided monarch, Henry VIII, who destroyed the tradition when he dissolved the monasteries, yet there were still vines in existence—at Hampton Court, for example, and at Arundel Castle. So it is not impossible, though for the first few years I began to wonder. Six bad harvests in a row and nothing to show for my labours but a few bottles of sickly verjus.' His face was dark with bitterness. 'But now at last I believe my luck has turned. Last year and the year before we had good autumn weather and the yield was excellent—a sparkling golden wine not so very different from the champagne produced in my own region of France.'

'Of course!' Lucy turned to him, her eyes bright with comprehension. 'I believe, Monsieur, I may have sampled some of your wine last night—at the Talbot Inn at Cuckfield . . .'

He nodded briefly. 'That is possible. We supply Tom Best with a few cases so that its quality may be appreciated by his customers, who will then spread the word abroad. Though the English seem oddly reluctant to admit that any wine produced in their own country need not be inferior to that of France . . .'

'But I think it is a wonderful achievement!' Lucy gazed once more out of the window, her eyes misting slightly at the sight of those devotedly tended vines. It struck her as both sad and romantic that this Frenchman should try to recreate, in his adopted country, the life he had been forced to leave behind him, against such tremendous odds.

For a moment M. de Sevignac stood watching her, an inscrutable expression on his face. Then he turned abruptly to face the room and said, 'Perhaps you had better sit down, Miss—'

'Mrs Forster,' Lucy supplied, seating herself on the edge of a sofa heavily encrusted with ormulu oakleaves.

'Ah, yes—Junot tells me you are a widow.' He sounded dubious. 'You must have married very young.'

'I was seventeen.'

'And your husband was killed soon after your marriage?'

'We had a month together, that is all.'

'But no child?'

Sharply into Lucy's mind intruded the image of her father saying, 'Thank God at least you had no children!' He had disapproved strongly of her marriage to William and would have done his best to prevent it had he not been so grievously ill at the time. Aloud she said, 'No, Monsieur. We did not have a child.'

'No matter. That may not have been your fault.'

Startled, she glanced enquiringly at him, but he only leaned further back in his chair and regarded her with an impassive look. Firmly she said, 'Monsieur, I was given to understand by Junot you are in need of a housekeeper, and it so happens that I am at this moment looking for employment. I came to Sussex to take up a post as governess, but for some reason it was decided that I should not be suitable. Why this was so I cannot explain, for I do not understand it myself, but I assure you it had nothing to do with my honesty—or rather lack of it. I can provide the highest references—'

'Mrs Forster, shall we cut short this charade? You know very well why you would not suit as a governess and I can easily imagine why Lady Stansgate did not wish to have you in her employ. The same reason makes you equally unsuitable as a housekeeper.'

Lucy turned pale. 'I do not know what you mean, Monsieur.'

'Do you seriously imagine that a young woman like yourself could take up residence here, in this house with me, and not provoke malicious gossip?'

'There is Junot—and Mrs Thrupp . . .'

'Junot is my servant and Mollie Thrupp is neither here nor there. In the eyes of the world, Mrs Forster, they simply would not count.' Through narrowed eyes he watched her closely. 'On the other hand, if we were to be married—'

Lucy rose to her feet and said coldly, 'We seem to be the victims, Monsieur, of some misunderstanding.'

'You may be, but not I.' He fixed her with a scornful look. 'Where is your commonsense, Mrs Forster? Obviously you have nowhere else to go and I am offering you both a house to run and the protection of my name. It is, incidentally, a name of some consequence—'

'I am sure it is,' she interrupted hastily. 'But why,

Monsieur, are you so anxious to find a wife? It seems to me you have been perfectly content until now without one . . .' Her gaze rested pointedly on the thick layer of dust coating the fire-dogs in the grate.

'I had no choice, Madame. It is only six months since I received the intelligence that my first wife had died. Until that time I was not free to look for another and since then I have been too busy with my vineyard, as I explained.'

'Even so, you have lived in this country for some years now. Surely during that time you must have made acquaintance—perhaps even formed an attachment—with a lady from some local family, rather than look to a total stranger?'

'Attachments—or even acquaintanceships—have little to do with the matter.' His tone was distant. 'My requirements in a wife are somewhat unusual, to say the least. A young woman of delicate upbringing would be of no use to me whatsoever.'

Lucy said unthinkingly, 'So you instructed Junot to find you a wife of "good yeoman stock"—?'

He gave her a piercing look. 'Quite so. It is true, Madame, that your appearance does not entirely fit my preconceived ideas. Nonetheless you answer my requirements in most other respects.' He made a sudden impatient movement. 'I wish you would sit down again, Mrs Forster. I find it exceedingly tiring to converse with someone who persists in standing over me like an avenging angel.'

Reluctantly Lucy sat down. 'Very well, but I must tell you that none of your reasonable arguments will make the slightest difference. In England, Monsieur, we have the greatest aversion to marriage between complete strangers.'

'I cannot imagine why. It seems to me a most logical arrangement—provided, of course, that one sees marriage as a contract between two people designed to bring them mutual advantages, as I believe would be the case if you and I were to marry.'

'A contract . . . ?' she repeated wonderingly.

'Precisely so. What I am offering you, Madame, is a solution to your problems—and one, moreover, which will ensure that you are adequately provided for during the rest of your lifetime—a consideration apparently overlooked by your first husband.' She made as if to interrupt him but he raised a hand to silence her. 'Oh, I do not pretend that this would be in any way a quixotic gesture on my part. Far from it. I should doubtless benefit far more than you from the arrangement.'

'But I do not *know* you, Monsieur,' she said in some desperation, beginning to feel that her arguments sounded like mere quibbles in the face of his determined reasoning.

'That is true. And you are naturally concerned lest I should turn out to be a wife-beater or a drunkard. I have only Junot to vouch for my character, though I suppose I could direct you to my cousin, but since he is himself a drunkard as well as a lecher I doubt the interview would reassure you. There is also my grandmother, but she would probably do her utmost to prevent our marriage on quite other grounds so that is hardly likely to aid my cause either. However—'

'Stop, I implore you!' Lucy pressed her hands to her ears. 'This is ridiculous! I cannot allow you to go on.'

'I see nothing ridiculous in it. If you would only set aside your idealistic and somewhat juvenile approach to marriage I think you would realise I have made a most practical suggestion.'

'It still seems to me,' Lucy persisted, 'that a house-keeper would suit your purpose equally well.'

'A housekeeper would do well enough as a temporary arrangement,' he conceded. 'But in that case I should look for a much older woman, and of quite different appearance.' A gleam of amusement appeared for the first time in his eyes. 'Strange as it may seem to you, Madame, I am not entirely immune to the gossip that my presence here—and my activities—' he waved a hand in the direction of the vineyard—'have already aroused. For several reasons I have no wish to give my neighbours cause to regard me as being even further beyond the pale than they already do. Perhaps that surprises you?'

Lucy shook her head, although in truth it did surprise her a little. She would have judged him a man who did not give a fig for what anyone thought of him.

'Come, Mrs Forster, we are wasting time.' He rose to his feet. 'I shall give you one hour to consider, while Junot is showing you round the house. At the end of that time I shall require an answer—yes or no.'

CHAPTER
THREE

'OH, whatever have you done, m'dear . . . ?' Mrs Best's voice was deeply troubled.

Lucy faced her across the kitchen table at the Talbot and tried to keep her gaze steady. 'I had no choice, Mrs Best. There is nowhere else for me to go. And it is only a contract, a way of protecting my good name as well as M. de Sevignac's. The French call it a marriage of convenience. Such arrangements are quite common . . .' Her voice tailed away unconvincingly.

Mrs Best shook her head. 'I've never heard the like before. Mind, I'm not saying I know aught against his character. Junot, indeed, sings his praises night and day. But Brooktye is a rough sort of a place for a lady like yourself—'

'The house is filthy,' Lucy agreed. 'But that is why he needs someone to care for it. And it could be beautiful . . .' Her eyes grew wistful. 'The moment I saw it I knew it was the sort of house I had always dreamed of. I fell in love with it, Mrs Best, and with the countryside . . .'

'*And* with Mr de Sevignac?'

'Of course not!' Lucy looked at her reproachfully. Then she added, choosing her words with care, 'Though I daresay I shall come to like him well enough in time.'

Mrs Best pressed her lips together. 'We must certainly hope so.' She gave Lucy a shrewd look. 'Of course, there are those who say that when his family escaped from France they brought with them a horde of valuable jewels, gold and silver, which he now keeps in a secret hiding-place at Brooktye.'

'I find that very difficult to believe,' said Lucy, refus-ing to let her mind dwell on the paradox of that opulent drawing-room. 'It is the kind of legend that country people often weave around strangers, especially fore-igners. He does not even *own* the house! Junot ex-plained to me that it was leased from his cousin—'

'Aye, and you know who that cousin is!' interrupted Mrs Best. 'Indeed, it would not surprise me to learn that the Frenchman intends to marry you partly to annoy Sir Ralph—or rather, his wife. I can just imagine how angry she will be to learn that the young woman she turned away as governess is to be married to her husband's cousin!'

'You cannot mean Lady Stansgate?' queried Lucy, turning pale.

Mrs Best saw her obvious consternation and softened her tone. 'We all guessed, m'dear, who was the grand lady who had treated you so badly. Who else could it be? The Stansgates are by far the biggest landowners in these parts.'

Lucy was silent, cursing her own stupidity. Of course the farm would be leased from Sir Ralph Stansgate. At last she said, 'It is strange that M. de Sevignac made no mention of the fact.'

'But then he's a strange man, to say the least.' Mrs Best moved nearer and took hold of her arm. 'Change your mind, m'dear. It's not too late.'

'But what else can I do?' Lucy regarded her steadily. 'Have *you* heard of any other position I might apply for?'

'Not yet. But you are welcome to stay here until you find something more suitable . . .'

'I cannot do that. It might be weeks before I find something else, and then at best it could only be as governess or companion to some elderly lady. At Brook-tye I shall at least be mistress of my own household and I have no doubt that M. de Sevignac is so little interested in domestic affairs he will give me a free rein to make what improvements I will. Give me a month, Mrs Best, and you will not know Brooktye!'

Mrs Best sighed deeply. 'I only hope you know what you are about. For all you're a widow you are still very young, m'dear. And he *is* a Frenchman . . .'

Lucy smiled. 'I can take care of myself, Mrs Best. You have no need to fear on my behalf.'

As she climbed the stairs to her room she reflected it was inevitable that local folk should regard M. de Sevignac, with his vineyard and his supposed store of treasure, as mad. To her he had seemed sane enough, if a little sombre in his manner; hardly once had a smile lightened his countenance in the course of their interview. On the other had, had he presented a more dashing, cheerful image, would she not have been instinctively on her guard? No, it was his very seriousness that had convinced her of his sincerity.

When Junot called later in the morning it was to inform her that the wedding had been fixed for the following Saturday afternoon, and would take place quietly in the church whose tall spire she could see from her window at the Talbot. Lucy was a little shocked to find that the ceremony was to be so soon, but realised that as far as M. de Sevignac was concerned there was no point in delaying the matter, especially as he was now paying the cost of her accommodation at the Talbot.

During the day the Reverend Fearon arrived to make her acquaintance and assure her that all was proceeding smoothly. 'How glad I am,' he remarked, bestowing on her an admiring look, 'that some good fortune has at last come to M. de Sevignac! I remember well the day that he arrived in Cuckfield with his wife and father. Such a tragedy, to lose them both.' He shook his head sadly. 'He has worked hard to make a life for himself in this country—so hard I have at times feared for his state of health. But now his achievements are to be crowned at last with the acquisition of a wife—and a very beautiful one, if I may be permitted to say so.'

Lucy accepted the compliment with a modest blush, reflecting that plainly Mr Fearon had no idea of the precise manner in which M. de Sevignac had acquired a wife.

'Now to practical matters,' he went on. 'M. de Sevignac suggested that I approach you personally for such details as date and place of birth. You are a widow, I believe? It would seem that you, too, have not been spared the blows of a cruel Fate . . .'

Lucy outlined the circumstances of her all-too-brief first marriage and William's sad end of the battlefield.

'Forgive me for asking,' said Mr Fearon gently, 'but I presume that his death was confirmed by the War Office?'

'Yes, indeed. I received a visit from one of his officers, who brought me a bag containing his—his personal possessions.' Lucy's voice broke a little as she recalled those few pathetic items, all that she had left to remind her of William.

'Of course, of course,' he murmured, going on quickly to say, 'I understand that the ceremony is to be a quiet one in view of the fact that you have both been married before—and, of course, that he is a Catholic—'

'Oh, my goodness!' said Lucy, startled. 'I never thought—'

If Mr Fearon was surprised that she should be unaware of her future husband's religious persuasions he gave no sign, but continued calmly, 'That, however, is no impediment in your case since it seems he has to some extent turned his back on his faith as well as his country and is quite willing to accept the tenets of the Anglican church.' He gave a resigned shrug. 'He says that as he is forced to be an Englishman he may as well accept the laws imposed by an English God. Not perhaps an ideal philosophy from my point of view, but at least it simplifies matters where your marriage is concerned. So—' he concluded briskly, 'there we are, Mrs Forster. I shall look forward to seeing you in church on Saturday.'

She shook hands with him formally, wondering what he would say if he knew the truth. Perhaps he would even refuse to marry them?

Time passed so slowly on the morning of her wedding that she went out to walk around the town. She gazed wistfully into the draper's bow-fronted window. There were many fine India cottons and muslins, silk scarves and Kashmir shawls, bows and rosettes. If only she could afford to buy something new—a length of yellow ribbon, perhaps, to make her old brown bonnet look more festive . . . But it was useless. She had no money of her own and plainly her future husband had none to spare for such idle fripperies. In any case he cared nothing for her appearance: he had said as much to Junot. His sole reason for marrying her was to improve his domestic arrangements and he obviously regarded the marriage service as a tiresome ceremony to be gone through with as little fuss as possible.

With a sigh she turned away and was about to cross the road when she saw a carriage approaching. Catching a glimpse of its occupant she hastily sought refuge in a doorway, but she need not have worried. Lady Stansgate wore a look of haughty unconcern and glanced neither to right not to left, presenting a faultless profile to the inhabitants of Cuckfield, who doffed their caps dutifully and continued to pass the time of day with each other—save for one man who spat derisively into the roadway and uttered a few oaths under his breath. But he was drunk, as was evident by the way he lurched across the pavement, knocking against Lucy's arm so violently that she dropped her reticule.

For a moment she feared he had thievery in mind, but as he swayed before her, making no attempt to snatch it from the ground, she realised it was nothing but an accident and bent to pick it up herself. The man, whose unkempt appearance proclaimed him some kind of vagrant, stood watching her, but she was careful to avoid looking directly at him and hurried away from the scene, aware that he was calling something after her.

As soon as she was certain he had not followed her she slowed again, thankful that he had not after all been a snatch-thief . . . Heaven knew she had little enough in her purse to steal! On the other hand, she was carrying a small travelling pistol of her father's, which had seemed a wise precaution while journeying about the countryside unaccompanied, and any vagrant might have been delighted to put his hands on *that*.

Safely back in her room at the Talbot she stared at herself in the looking-glass, wishing she possessed something more suitable to wear than Kitty's gown. Yet the weather was still far from warm and her only other gowns were either too lightweight or too plain. The redingote had at least been fashionable once, even if she no longer felt entirely comfortable in it. Thankfully M. De Sevignac did not appear to be tarred with the same brush as Sir Ralph Stansgate! Indeed, he had given no indication whatsoever that he had even noticed the slim waist and rounded bosom so embarrassingly emphasised by the bronze velvet.

Her mind went back to her first wedding morning and she saw instead a vision of herself at seventeen, dressed in pale blue muslin and breathless with excitement and fear. Yes—fear; because she was going against her father's wishes and it had seemed somehow callous to marry while he lay on his death-bed with his breath rasping cruelly in his chest. Bronchial pneumonia, the doctor said, and very little chance he would recover. How wicked of her to dress so frivolously with flowers in her hair, and run to the man he mistrusted! But William had been so anxious that they should be wed before the forces assembling on the Kentish Downs were ordered to sail for Holland. He was a Militiaman, one of the thousands who had accepted the offer of a £10 bounty and were drafted into a regular regiment to be sent on active service abroad, for which they were ill-prepared. The 'Bounty soldiers' many called them. How handsome he had looked in his uniform! Lucy had been head over ears in love for the first time in her young life, and it was hardly surprisingly if the dictates of her heart proved more powerful than her sense of duty to her father.

But in the end it was William who died, whilst her father made a miraculous recovery and went to recuperate in Bath, where he met and married Kitty Mulliner within two months.

The vision faded and left her staring at a pale-faced young woman who bore little resemblance to that innocent, eager bride of six years ago. Smoothing down her ever-wayward hair, she regarded herself critically and was not ill-pleased with what she saw. M. de Sevignac was not getting such a bad bargain, she thought; as yeoman wives went she was definitely above average. She smiled wryly to herself.

Of the service itself Lucy remembered little, except for two moments of mild surprise. The first came when she heard for the first time her husband's full name, Philippe Amédée Raoul de Sevignac; and the second when he slipped a band of plain gold on to her finger and she saw it next to the other wedding ring, which she had carelessly omitted to remove. The new ring shone deeply and made the old look somehow dull and tawdry. No doubt William's ring had been of inferior gold because it was all

he could afford, she thought unemotionally as the Vicar
spoke the words of the blessing over them; but where did
this ring come from? That secret horde, allegedly hidden
somewhere at Brooktye? Somehow she doubted it, but
had to acknowledge there was much she did not understand about her new husband's way of life.

She glanced up at his dark, forbidding countenance
and caught him looking down at her with an expression
that made her heart miss a beat, a gleam of speculative
interest mixed with something else she could not define.
But it was quickly veiled and she decided it must have
been a trick of the light slanting through the narrow
window. Nonetheless it sowed a seed of unease in her
mind which made it difficult to concentrate on the
remainder of the ceremony.

Outside the churchyard a little crowd had gathered,
leaning over the wall to watch them emerge. Obviously
the word had spread that the Frenchman was taking a
wife, but they were for the most part silent observers,
content merely to look on and make their own judgments.

Their return to Brooktye was clouded by the discov-
ery of Mollie Thrupp sitting in the middle of the kitchen
floor with cap awry and smelling strongly of rum. 'Get
up, woman!' said Junot in disgust, pushing his toe
against her backside. 'Get up and do your duty.'

'Wedding day!' Mrs Thrupp announced in a slurred,
sing-song voice. 'Bless the bride . . .' She burst into a fit
of uncontrolled laughter.

'Mrs Thrupp,' said Lucy quietly. 'Please stand up and
try to pull yourself together.'

With difficulty Mollie struggled to her feet and stood
in front of them defiantly. 'And just who d'yer think you
are, my fine lady, coming in here and ordering me about
in me own kitchen? I *tole* you already, we don't need you
here. We was doing all right afore you come—wasn't we,

Junot?' She flung a plump, golden arm round Junot's neck and he reeled momentarily under the unexpected weight.

'It is foolish to behave so,' he told her sternly. 'It will not please Monsieur—'

'Oh, I know how to please Monsewer, don't you worry!' said Mollie, pouting her full lips. 'Leastways I pleased him well enough till *she* came poking her nose in.'

Lucy flushed. She found the notion of M. de Sevignac taking pleasure in this coarse, slatternly creature peculiarly distasteful, though she could hardly have supposed him to live a totally celibate existence.

A maudlin tear ran down Mollie's cheek. 'Where's she come from, anyway? Putting on airs and graces, like she was a lady—but she don't fool *me*! There's summat amiss, else why would she—?'

During this speech M. de Sevignac had entered the kitchen. 'That's enough, Mollie,' he warned. 'I think perhaps you had better leave us until you are quite recovered.'

She glowered at him, pushing her hair out of her eyes. 'Oh, I'm leaving you all right. And I shan't come back— not while she's here!' She stabbed a finger at Lucy.

Lucy could not help feeling overjoyed at this threat, but she tried to keep it from showing in her face.

With swaying hips Mollie Thrupp walked unsteadily to the door, pausing only to say over her shoulder, 'But you ain't heard the last of me, so don't think you have!' The sound of the door slamming behind her was followed by a sudden squawking of chickens, disturbed by her erratic progress across the yard.

As if anxious to smooth over the awkwardness of this incident, Junot stepped forward and begged her to come into the dining-room, where he had prepared a simple wedding breakfast in her honour. Gratefully Lucy followed him into an attractive room, low-ceilinged, white-walled and sunny, the only furniture a mahogany table desperately in need of polish, several matching chairs upholstered in threadbare silk of an indeterminate colour and a sideboard covered with burns and ring-marks—all in direct contrast to the elegant pieces she had seen in the drawing-room. In this room, certainly, there was no sign of the first Madame de Sevignac's extravagant taste.

In a short while M. de Sevignac appeared, carrying a bottle of wine which he handed to Junot. 'Come now, we must toast the bride,' he said impatiently, 'and then we can all return to our business.'

Lucy accepted the glass of wine, smiled dutifully as Junot proposed her health and happiness in the most flowery of phrases that would doubtless have sounded better in his native tongue, and reflected with some amusement that she might well be the only bride in England to spend most of her wedding day with a duster in one hand and a dish-mop in the other. As soon as she had eaten a slice of the cake Junot had baked especially for the occasion and washed it down with a glass of the sparkling wine, she made her way briskly to the door. 'I will leave you now to unpack my valise, Monsieur. If Junot will show me which is my room . . . ?'

'Of course.' M. de Sevignac bowed politely.

Before she could reach the door, however, she was arrested by the sound of horses' hooves in the yard outside and the strident shouts of a coachman calling 'Whoa!' combined with a confusion of other voices.

M. de Sevignac frowned and told Junot in French to discover immediately the cause of this disturbance. 'If it is who I think it is,' he added, 'on no account allow them to enter.'

Such instructions proved useless, however, for when Junot tried to leave the room he was swept aside by the elegant figure of Lady Stansgate, attired in violet silk with a parasol to match and a mass of purple plumes decorating her bonnet.

Lucy stared at her in dismay. Lady Stansgate's gaze travelled rapidly over the scene, taking in the wedding-cake on the mahogany table and the empty wine-glasses, and came to rest on Lucy. 'So it is true,' she said softly, turning upon M. de Sevignac a look of bitter reproach. 'How *could* you, Philippe?'

He returned her look steadily but made no attempt to defend himself.

Without turning her head Lady Stansgate addressed the man who had entered the room behind her. 'You see, Ralph? I was right—your cousin has taken a wife and not seen fit to invite even his own family to the wedding. And no wonder, since he has married the designing female whom I refused to have in my house as a governess!'

Sir Ralph advanced into the room and began eyeing Lucy up and down with eyes like hot gooseberries. 'And one can see why, my dear,' he remarked at last. 'Such good looks would have been shockingly wasted in the schoolroom.'

He cut a handsome figure, dressed in a chocolate-brown frock coat cut away in the front to reveal a slight tendency to paunchiness, and was undoubtedly the man she had seen on the stairs at Stansgate Park. A pair of pudding-faced girls followed him into the room and stood behind their mama, giggling slyly with each other as they took in the scene.

Sir Ralph turned to M. de Sevignac. 'Congratulations, coz. Once again you have found yourself a beauty to wed—though this one, I fancy, may prove rather more compliant than the first.' He made a gallant bow towards Lucy, but as he took her hand and began to raise it to his lips Lady Stansgate's parasol came down viciously on his arm and he stepped back with an oath.

At the same instant M. de Sevignac moved forward, apparently quite recovered from his surprise and with a purposeful gleam in his eye. 'This is an unexpected honour,' he said with heavy irony. 'My wife and I are delighted to welcome you to Brooktye. We did not invite you to the wedding because we had not realised you would be so anxious to come. It was a very quiet affair—'

'A clandestine affair, you mean,' interrupted Lady Stansgate. 'My dear Philippe, it is less than a week since I turned that woman out of my house.'

'A whirlwind romance, indeed,' observed Sir Ralph, smiling.

'Romance!' Lady Stansgate's eyes rested coldly on Lucy. 'I don't doubt you came straight here and wove some fiction about how badly you had been treated so that poor Philippe felt obliged to offer you a home. From there it would be a simple matter for a woman of your type—' She broke off, biting her lip in vexation; then turned again on M. de Sevignac. 'Have you considered how this will upset your grandmother? I take it you have not informed her?'

'No, but I am sure *you* intend doing so at the earliest opportunity.' Calmly he picked up the bottle of wine and said, 'Junot, furnish our guests with glasses so that they may toast our health. And you had best fetch two more bottles from the cellar . . .'

'We are not staying!' Lady Stansgate turned towards the door. 'Come, Ambrosine. Seraphina.'

Her husband, however, had already accepted the glass offered to him and was regarding the contents thoughtfully. 'Wait for me in the carriage, my dear. I have a mind to become better acquainted with the bride.'

Lady Stansgate regarded her husband with astonished contempt. 'You may do as you please, Ralph, but I have seen quite enough. The woman is, as I thought, an adventuress.' She almost choked on the words. 'And as for you—' Turning to M. de Sevignac she shook her head and said brokenly, 'Oh, Philippe—how could you allow yourself to be tricked into making such an—an *impossible* marriage?' As if she could not bear to look at him for another instant, she swept from the room, her daughters trailing in her wake.

Sir Ralph sipped tentatively at the wine and then relaxed. 'Thank God! For one moment I thought you meant to feed me some of that dishwater you brew yourself. This is excellent. What is it?'

M. de Sevignac smiled. 'Last year's dishwater. The first tasting in honour of this significant occasion.'

Sir Ralph stared at his glass for a full three seconds before bursting into loud laughter. 'But it is *good*, Philippe! And grown on my own land—I can hardly believe it. Send over a hog's head to the Park and I will try it on my guests. Could put you in business.'

The cousins regarded each other almost amicably, as if the removal of Lady Stansgate's presence from the room had lightened the atmosphere. Sir Ralph strolled over to the window to survey the vineyard and accepted another glass of wine. 'Fascinating,' he murmured. 'Quite fascinating. Did you know, Philippe, that locally your wine is known as Frenchman's Gold?'

M. de Sevignac permitted himself a smile. 'No, I did not know.'

'Yet your grapes are red. I confess I am ignorant in these matters but I should have expected the wine also to be red.'

M. de Sevignac explained. 'When I began I had only two varieties of grape—the Auvernat and the Pinot Meunier, both of which were cuttings I managed to procure here. The first wine I produced from them was red, but it was so rough and harsh that is was quite undrinkable. Nonetheless, through the harshness I detected a flavour that reminded me of the wine we used to produce in France, so I experimented and discovered to my surprise that I had created a white wine that was much more palatable. During the Peace, when Junot and I travelled to France, we brought back with us some more cuttings—*pied rouge, sauvoir* and *muscat rouge et blanc*. These are the young vines you see now.'

'I used to think you were mad, Philippe—but now I am not so sure.' Sir Ralph drained his glass and turned his attention once more to Lucy. 'Regretfully, Madame, I must take my leave of you and wish you joy. Do you speak, by the way? So far I have not heard you say a word.'

With a shock Lucy realised that she had not in fact uttered a single syllable since Lady Stansgate made her dramatic entrance into the room. 'Yes, I do speak, Sir Ralph—and often speak my mind, which is, I am afraid, how I may have incurred Lady Stansgate's disapproval.'

He regarded her enigmatically. 'I doubt it was your speech that annoyed her, my dear. May I kiss the bride, coz?'

She was aware that M. de Sevignac, standing beside her, had stiffened, but he spoke calmly enough. 'If the bride does not object . . .'

She closed her eyes as Sir Ralph's face loomed nearer to her own and endured the brief, moist pressure of his lips on hers.

'Delightfully fresh,' he murmured. 'Once again I find myself envying you, Philippe. You do have the damnedest luck.'

'I will escort you to the door.'

After the departure of the carriage Lucy looked for an opportunity to ask her husband if her summary dismissal from Stansgate Park had in any way influenced his decision to offer her a home. She also wanted to know if his grandmother was indeed that fearsome old lady who had raised her eyeglass to scrutinise her as she was driven through the grounds? And why had Lady Stansgate behaved as though his marriage were almost a *personal* insult to herself? Perhaps she cherished a secret tendresse for her cousin-by-marriage, though certainly there had been no suggestion the feeling was mutual.

His family history intrigued her and she would like to know more; but no such opportunity presented itself. It was almost as if he were avoiding her, and when at last he joined Junot and herself in the kitchen for a mug of chocolate he looked so tired and drawn she decided the matter had better wait for a more auspicious moment.

It was with some relief that she at length excused herself and went up to her bedchamber. It was a stark room, furnished only with a bed, a table and a chest with a mirror so dark and spotted with age it was impossible to make out one's reflection at all clearly. She made ready for bed, smiling to herself as she donned the nightgown of plain lawn with a demure trim of lace around the neck. Hardly a suitable garment for a wedding night! But this, of course, was no ordinary wedding night . . .

What if it were? The thought brought a warm flush to her cheeks. Supposing M. de Sevignac should after all demand his marital rights, despite their agreement? If he should force her, against her will, what chance could she possibly have against a man of his height and muscular build? William had been of much slighter stature. He had made love with great gentleness, almost as if he were afraid of frightening her. Somehow she had the feeling M. de Sevignac's lovemaking would be entirely different . . .

Briefly she closed her eyes, feeling a little dizzy; then chided herself for being foolish. Of course he would abide by the terms of their agreement! She had recognised him at once as a man of honour, whatever his faults—otherwise she would not have married him.

Nonetheless she took out the small brass-barrelled pistol and slipped it into the drawer of the table beside the bed, together with the cloth bag from her valise containing the bullets and powder flask. That done, she leapt quickly into bed, blew out the candle and slid beneath the covers.

She had only just begun to drift off to sleep when a knock at the door brought her swiftly back to consciousness. Raising her head from the pillow, she was astonished to see M. de Sevignac enter, carrying a lamp and clad only in his breeches with a loose white shirt unbuttoned at the neck. Startled, she stared at him incredulously. 'Yes, Monsieur?'

He kicked the door to behind him and set the lamp down on the chest, not saying a word.

Lucy drew the sheets up to her chin. 'Monsieur, I do not understand . . .'

The bed creaked as he sat on the edge to remove his boots.

'Monsieur!' Lucy sat up, her hair tumbling about her shoulders. 'Will you please leave my room immediately?'

He turned his head to look at her, frowning slightly. 'But we are married, Madame. Have you forgotten already?'

'A marriage of convenience only,' she reminded him, her voice shaking a little. 'A contract between two people, to bring them—er, mutual benefit, you said.'

'Precisely.' He put out a hand as if to pull the sheet away from her chin but she held on to it all the more fiercely. 'Come, Madame—such modesty is charming but there is no need to overdo it. We have, after all, both been married before.'

'That was quite different,' she protested. 'This time

there was no question of the marriage being other than a—a civil contract, an arrangement to protect both my good name and yours.'

'It was contracted in church, Madame,' he said quietly. 'Once again you seem to have been under a misapprehension. I certainly never intended this to be a marriage in name only and among the mutual benefits I had in mind were my rights as a husband. I am a man, Madame, who has been forced to live alone too long, and in taking a wife I looked also for a home and a family. Had it been merely a housekeeper I required then any hard-faced harridan would have suited my needs admirably. But those were not my instructions to Junot. And for once in his life—' His expression grew warmer as he looked at her eyes, enormous in the lamplight—'he showed remarkable good taste.'

Appalled, Lucy gazed at him, wondering how she could have been so naive. 'But I do not *know* you—!' she stuttered helplessly.

'Then allow me to introduce myself. I am your husband.'

'Oh, this is impossible. I came here only as a housekeeper . . . You persuaded me into marriage on the grounds it would avoid gossip, but instead you—'

'Oh, come!' he interrupted with a grim smile. 'You surely cannot accuse me of forcing you to marry me against your will? No, my dear—it suited you as well as it did me. A widow for six years—? You have no need to pretend with me . . .' With a quick wrench he pulled back the covers. She opened her mouth to scream, but he covered it with his hand and muttered, 'Don't be such a fool—and stop play-acting!'

His other hand was already pulling at the ties of her nightgown, only to find them securely fastened. Taking advantage of this respite, Lucy tried to twist away from his grasp but it seemed her struggles only served to increase his determination. With an impatient oath he ripped the thin fabric downwards, exposing her breasts.

As Lucy felt his warm lips against her bare flesh a strange sense of helplessness flooded through her veins, weakening her resolve. What was the use of fighting, when his strength was so much greater than hers? Her limbs felt heavy, overcome with langour. She gave a low moan—half anguish, half pleasure.

Sensing her sudden acquiescence he raised his head to stare down at her, taking his hand from her mouth to push her tousled hair back from her forehead in a curiously tender gesture. Then he crushed his lips to hers, parting them hungrily in a deep, searching kiss. Lucy felt a shiver of excitement run through her treacherous body. Reluctantly she found herself responding, her arms creeping around his neck of their own volition, her hands spreading against his broad, muscular back, pressing him closer. It was so long since a man held her in his arms . . . Perhaps her memory was playing her false for she could have sworn she had never felt like this before, every nerve in her body tingling with awareness. But then of course with William she had been only a young girl, loving but shy and a little timid . . .

William!

A wave of shame and remorse swept over her. How could she betray his memory in such a shameless fashion? This madness, this fever that possessed her now had nothing to do with love—not the pure and gentle love she had known with William. The hands even now caressing her, rousing her to new heights of passion, belonged to a stranger—a man she had met only once before today! Feebly she pushed against his chest, turning her head aside in self-disgust, but he seemed oblivious to her protests. In a moment, she realised with horror, it would be too late . . .

Only then did she remember the gun. Desperately she stretched out a hand to touch the table, then moved her fingers down until she found the handle of the drawer. She gave it a tug. It came open so abruptly that she wondered he had not noticed the movement, but fortunately he was far too preoccupied. Gathering all her resolve she grasped the pistol and brought it up against his ribs, jabbing so hard he could be left in no doubt as to the nature of her threat. With her lips close to his ear she hissed, 'Leave me alone—or I shall kill you!'

For a second he froze, then drew back to look with astonishment at the pistol, now held steadily between her two hands and pointing at his chest. His gaze returned to her eyes, fixed and desperate in her pale face.

With a deceptive lack of haste he rose to his feet, calmly adjusting his clothing. 'Well, Madame,' he murmured. 'I must confess you had me completely fooled. For a moment there I could have sworn—' With a rapid movement he bent forward and closed his fingers firmly over her own, forcing her to release her grip on the pistol.

Once it was in his own hands he looked down and smiled wryly. 'A useful-looking weapon—but, as I thought, not even primed.' With a contemptuous gesture he threw it on the bed. 'However, you need have no further fears. I would not dream of forcing myself upon a woman who likes me so little she is prepared to kill me rather than suffer my lovemaking. It is, I must admit, something of a novel experience for me.' Picking up the lamp he turned to the door, but on reaching it he hesitated and looked back at her as she lay against the pillows, clutching her tattered nightgown to her breasts. An odd expression flitted across his face and when he spoke again it was in a quieter, almost conciliatory tone. 'I am sorry, Madame. The life I lead made me rough and impatient, unused to considering the sensibilities of a

lady like yourself. Of course you are right. We need time
to become better acquainted. So—regretfully—I will bid
you goodnight.'

He closed the door softly behind him, leaving Lucy
staring at it with a confusing mixture of emotions which
would allow her little sleep that night.

CHAPTER
FOUR

THE next morning Lucy rose early, donned her plainest, most workmanlike gown of grey kerseymere and set to work with determined vigour, allowing no time for her thoughts to dwell on the events of the previous evening. She could not help feeling apprehensive at the prospect of confronting M. de Sevignac, particularly since she was conscious of vague stirrings of guilt. Perhaps she *had* leapt too quickly to the wrong conclusions about his proposal of marriage: after all, it was a reasonable enough ambition for any man to have children of his own, especially as his first marriage had proved unfruitful. She had an uneasy feeling she had not given the matter enough thought; but as to the matter of his behaviour last night she dared not give any thought at all, for she found the recollection far too disturbing. So instead she scrubbed and polished, swept and dusted, and thanked heaven that M. de Sevignac seemed far too busy in his vineyard this morning to pay any attention to his new wife.

When the kitchen was restored to a reasonable state of order she turned her attention to the rest of the house, taking down grimy curtains to be washed, opening windows in unused rooms to let in the fresh spring air and vigorously beating rugs and carpets, an occupation she found particularly satisfying if she directed her thoughts to Lady Stansgate while doing it.

'I have made out a list of things we need when next you go into Cuckfield,' she informed Junot, when he put his head round the kitchen door. 'I fear it is a long one, but the larder is woefully bare.' A sudden thought struck her and she added doubtfully, 'Or is it that M. de Sevignac cannot afford—'

Junot gave a non-committal shrug. 'If they are necessary.'

'I believe that in the end it will prove more economical,' Lucy assured him earnestly. 'This morning I went down that passageway and discovered the most beautiful little dairy, where we could store bacon and sides of ham. Better still, perhaps one day we can return it to its proper use and produce our own butter and milk, like a real farm . . .' She saw the hurt expression on his face. 'I am sorry, Junot, but Brooktye has been allowed to fall into a sorry state. Even the chickens look neglected.'

'I know, Madame!' Junot spread his hands wide. 'But it is not my fault! I am not a farmer but a steward of the house—I do not know how you call it in English. Oh, I will clean out the stable and help Monsieur with the harvesting of the grapes because I must, but for me it is not at all natural, you understand?'

'Yes, I do understand.' Lucy sighed. She turned again to her list. 'Now, flour—there is plenty there, but most of it is damp and grey with age. Oh, and tea—there is not a tea-leaf to be found. I cannot comprehend how people can exist without tea!'

'Mollie Thrupp—sometimes she makes the tea,' said Junot doubtfully.

'In a quite horrid teapot which I have thrown away. So you had better add that to your list as well . . .'

She had taken it for granted that Mrs Thrupp meant what she said and would not be returning, so it was with a sense of dismay that she looked out of the window later in the morning and saw the woman coming up the drive. Resolutely she turned to face the door.

Mollie Thrupp entered, looking sullen but at least

completely sober. If the transformation that had taken place in the kitchen surprised her she gave no sign of it, but instead bent to stroke the one-eyed cat, curled up in its usual place on the range.

Lucy took a deep breath and said evenly, 'Good morning, Mrs Thrupp.'

''Morning,' came the terse answer; and then, as a reluctant afterthought, 'Ma'am.'

'As you may have noticed,' Lucy went on, 'I have already made a start on a thorough spring-clean of the house. However, I shall be glad of your help. Perhaps you would begin by polishing the dining-room table, while I set about sorting the linen. When you have finished that you can prepare some vegetables for this evening's meal. I thought perhaps a rabbit pie . . .' She looked doubtfully at Mollie, wondering if the woman was capable of producing anything remotely edible. Well, if not then *she* would have to roll up her sleeves and get on with it herself. Heaven knew she had spent enough time in the kitchen as a child, watching Cook make feather-light pastry that melted in the mouth.

Mrs Thrupp gave a brief nod. 'There's no lack of rabbits, what with his Lordship forever shooting at 'em in his vineyard.'

'Good,' said Lucy briskly. 'In that case we are not likely to die of starvation. Perhaps in time we may even aspire to something a little more ambitious.'

'He don't take much interest in food,' Mollie informed her with a scowl. 'Give him a bit o' bread and some broth and he don't complain.'

'*He* may not complain but *I* shall,' Lucy retorted firmly. 'From now on, Mrs Thrupp, I intend to make sure my husband eats at least one good meal a day.'

She left the kitchen, aware that Mollie was glaring at her venomously, but knew she must establish her au-

thority from the beginning. She could foresee their
relationship would be a stormy one; on the other hand, it
was not her wish to inflict hardship on the woman, who
had obviously returned because she needed the money.
After all, it was only yesterday that she herself had been
in the same desperate plight. Moreover, she could do
with the help. There was much to be done to set the
house to rights, and when that was achieved she intended turning her attention to the garden.

After sorting the bed-linen, which she found to be in
an indifferent state of repair, she tentatively opened the
door of M. de Sevignac's bedchamber and looked inside.
It was even starker than her own, almost monk-like in its
lack of material comfort. There were no pictures on the
walls or ornaments, the only object of note being a large
marquetry box on the dressing-table. She advanced into
the room to look at it more closely. Could such a box
hold the fabled treasure? Gently she tried the lid, but it
was locked. With a smile she admonished herself for
being ridiculous. No-one in their right senses would
store anything valuable in so obvious a place. All the
same, she was intrigued by its magnificence and decided
it must have come from France, one of the few relics of
his former life.

'Does Mollie Thrupp have a husband?' she asked
Junot later, when he was helping her polish a pair of
tarnished silver candlesticks she had discovered hidden
away in a cupboard.

'Not as far as one can tell.' He gave her a sly grin. 'But
she does not lack for company, you understand?'

'I do indeed.' Lucy suddenly had a vivid picture of
Mollie Thrupp in the arms of M. de Sevignac, her dark
hair streaming over his shoulders. Thrusting it out of her
mind, she went on hastily, 'Where does she live?'

'In an old cottage down by the gate. Perhaps you have
not notice—it is almost hidden behind the hedge. My

master lets her live there, and in return she comes to cook and clean for us.'

No doubt a most convenient arrangement all round, Lucy reflected, but it made the possibility of replacing Mollie by someone more suitable seem very remote. If the woman lost her position at Brooktye she would also lose her home, and that would be a cruel blow, no matter how ramshackle the cottage might be. 'Is she often drunk' she inquired.

'Once a week, maybe. It depends if anyone gives her the—' He broke off abruptly because Lucy had uttered a little scream and was staring out of the window. 'What is the matter, Madame?'

'There was a—a face. A face peering in at us . . .' Lucy recovered quickly and went over to the window to look out.

With a muttered exclamation Junot ran out of the door and into the yard, shouting and clapping his hands. Minutes later he came back, looking pleased with himself. 'He is gone! There is no need to fear—it was only a man who begs for food.' Angrily he rounded on Mollie who had followed him into the kitchen. 'I tell you not to feed that man! He is a nuisance, hanging about. Who knows what he will steal?'

Mollie gave him a sly grin. 'It was *her* he wanted,' she muttered, nodding at Lucy. 'He says he knows her.'

Lucy frowned, puzzled. 'I have certainly seen him before,' she told Junot. 'In Cuckfield, when he knocked against me in the street and I dropped my reticule. I thought at first he was a thief but he was only drunk. I wonder how he knew I was here . . . or what he wants?'

Junot swelled out his chest protectively. 'You are not to fear, Madame. I tell him if he comes again I will take him straight to my master.'

Mollie Thrupp gave a derisive snort. 'And he laughed! Threats don't worry Will Voller. He's too slippery by half, that one.' She glanced at Lucy. 'He'll be back, if there's summat he wants.'

Lucy turned away and went on with her polishing, but she could not help feeling disturbed. There was something about the man that made her uneasy, and it was not a pleasant thought that he had made it his business to find out where she lived.

Suddenly aware that her back and arms were aching from the unaccustomed effort she decided the time had come for a more restful task. From a writing desk in the drawing-room she took a pen and some paper she had discovered earlier when dusting: it was old but of good quality and smelled faintly of violets. It must have been the property, she thought, of the first Madame de Sevignac, but that did not trouble her in the least. She very much doubted that her husband was at all sentimental about his first wife's memory and suspected that the paper had remained in the desk through oversight rather than as a treasured keepsake. Sitting down, she wrote first to Mr Haverfield, advising him that she had not after all taken up residence at Stansgate Park but instead had found a position at Brooktye on the same estate. What he would make of that Heaven alone knew, but she suspected his main reaction would be relief that he need no longer feel responsible for her.

When that was done she wrote an almost identical letter to her father, in order to put his mind at rest where she was concerned, though she feared he might by now be too deep in his own misery to care what happened to any of them; and finally she wrote to her stepmother, saying she hoped Kitty would soon recover from the nervous decline into which the events of the last few months had plunged her. Into the same envelope she slipped a brief message to James, her half-brother, who was only five and whom she missed far more, if the truth must be told, than either Kitty or her father. The recollection of his tearful bewilderment when they parted was more than she could bear to remember, so determinedly she rose and took all the letters into the kitchen, intending to ask Junot to post them on his next visit to Cuckfield, but to her consternation she discovered M. de Sevignac in the act of helping himself to bread and cheese from the larder.

For a moment they stared at each other. The expression in his eyes was unreadable, but he looked exceedingly weary, the deep lines on either side of his mouth more pronounced than ever. Had he too spent a sleepless night? she wondered.

Lucy was the first to turn away. 'I am sorry,' she said in a low voice. 'If I had known you were hungry I would have asked Mrs Thrupp to prepare you some food.'

'This suits me well enough,' he said coolly.

She was suddenly conscious of her apron and the linen cloth still fastened over her hair like a nun's coif to protect her from the dust. 'I have made a start on the house,' she said nervously, 'though I fear I have as yet made little impression. There is so much to be done—' She faltered, aware that he had moved closer.

'Madame,' he began urgently, 'I must ask you to forgive me—'

'No, please!' Hot colour flooded into her cheeks and she kept her face averted. 'On thinking it over I realise it was partly my own fault for being so foolish as to think that you . . . that we . . .' His nearness confused her, recalling the strange weakness she had felt last night. She made an effort to control herself, pleating the folds of her apron with trembling fingers. 'Only it seemed rather sudden . . .'

'I should not have behaved as I did,' he said soberly. 'It's just that you were so—'

Whatever he meant to say was interrupted by the ominous sound of carriage-wheels rumbling down the rough track, followed by the stamping of hooves on the cobbled yard outside, in a less noisy repetition of yesterday's events.

'Damnation!' swore M. de Sevignac under his breath. 'We are become wondrous popular all of a sudden . . .'

The door burst open to admit a perspiring Junot, who broke into a torrent of French so rapid that Lucy had difficulty in following it. One thing was clear, however. M. de Sevignac's grandmother had arrived!

The effect of this news upon M. de Sevignac was remarkable. His face suddenly transformed with pleasure, he strode rapidly across the kitchen and disappeared into the yard. After only a second's hesitation Lucy followed him as far as the doorway. Today she was better prepared and had no intention of allowing herself to be intimidated again by a member of the Stansgate family.

In the courtyard stood not the landau she had seen before but a chaise. Still seated in the carriage, and having apparently no intention of descending from it, were two ladies, one the dowdy companion and the other Lady Emilie Stansgate, dressed in black crape decorated with a profusion of beads and feathers. Her hand was gallantly kissed by her grandson, after which he tried to persuade her to disembark.

'Thank you, no, Philippe,' said Lady Emilie in carrying tones. 'Having once crossed your threshold I have no desire ever to do so again. The squalor of your establishment is far too depressing! I have come only to discover for myself if what Letty tells me is true, that you have allowed yourself to be ensnared by a woman of low moral character whom she had already turned away from her door.' As she spoke her gaze travelled round the yard, took in Lucy standing on the doorstep and passed over her, as if expecting some quite different apparition to appear.

M. de Sevignac followed her glance and smiled. Going across to Lucy he took hold of her hand and led her towards his grandmother. 'Here she is, Grandmère—your woman of low moral character. My wife.'

This time it was Lady Emilie who was struck dumb, raising her eyeglass to take in every detail of Lucy's appearance, from apron and head-cloth to the smudge of dirt on her nose. M. de Sevignac, suddenly aware of his wife's drudge-like garb, made an impatient sound and roughly pulled the cloth from her head so that her hair sprang into vivid life.

Lady Emilie gazed at it and a gleam of amusement came into her eye. 'Ah! For a moment there I was confused, I must admit. But now I think I begin to understand a little. What is your name, child?'

Lucy dropped a slight curtsey, keeping her eyes fixed firmly on Lady Emilie's face. 'Lucy Forster, my lady.' Then, realising her mistake, she blushed. 'That is to say, I *was* Lucy Forster. Now I am—'

'Yes, yes, I'm perfectly well aware who you are now! But I have a fancy I've seen you before. Would that be possible?'

Lucy gave her ladyship a level look. 'Quite possible. As no doubt your granddaughter-in-law informed you, she had just interviewed me for the post of governess to her daughters and decided I would not be suitable. When you saw me I was on my way back to Cuckfield, with the intention of catching the next stage to London.'

'And what occurred, pray, to make you change your plans?'

Lucy hesitated before answering. 'Two things, my lady. The first was that I had nowhere to go in London, and the second that I met Junot—'

'—Who told her I had need of someone to run the house,' M. de Sevignac intercepted smoothly. 'An arrangement which happened to suit us both.'

'So I can imagine!' retorted Lady Emilie.

M. de Sevignac ignored the implication. 'I do wish you would come into the house, Grandmère. I think you would find it considerably improved. My wife has worked hard to make it more habitable.'

Lucy looked at him in surprise. She had not thought he had even noticed.

'Very well.' Lady Emilie threw off the woollen rug covering her knees and accepted her grandson's hand. 'You had best stay here, Prossett, or you will only get under our feet.' This was to her companion, who nodded meekly and gave a discreet sigh of relief. 'I suppose as usual I must enter by the back door . . .' As she reached it she paused to address Lucy over her shoulder. 'One of your first tasks, my dear, should be to set that lazy manservant about clearing a path to the front door. It is no sort of a proper establishment that obliges all its visitors to take on the habit of tradesmen!'

Behind her back Lucy's eyes met those of M. de Sevignac, almost as if they were conspirators, and she saw a light in his that looked suspiciously like triumph. So he too had noticed that 'my dear' and took it to be significant.

Lady Emilie's gaze passed rapidly over the kitchen, her sharp old eyes not missing a single detail of the transformation since last she had set foot inside it. 'So!' she murmured with a faint smile. Then she demanded, 'Well? Am I not to be shown the rest of the house? Kitchens are all very fine in their way, but they are not places on which I count myself an expert. My own I visit only once a year, at Christmas, when I make my annual inspection. I have a fancy to see what changes you have wrought in the other rooms.'

'There has not been time yet to do more than remove the dust and cobwebs,' said Lucy as she conducted Lady Emilie through the hall. M. de Sevignac seemed content to follow in silence and when they reached the drawing-room he leaned negligently against the mantelshelf, an attitude which drew Lucy's eyes to the mud still adhering to his boots.

Lady Emilie's gaze followed a similar course. 'Now that you have found a wife who intends to ensure you live in civilised surroundings,' she remarked with asperity, 'the least you can do, Philippe, is take some thought for your appearance and try to dress like a gentleman rather than a farm labourer—or a *vigneron*, if that is what you choose to call yourself. Go and change your boots this instant and leave me alone to talk to my new granddaughter-in-law.'

M. de Sevignac glanced downwards and flushed, rather like a small boy who has been chastised and knows it is well-deserved, but he bowed agreeably enough and backed towards the door. 'I will leave you alone, if that is what you wish, no doubt to tear my character to shreds. But may I put in one plea, Grand-mère, for an ounce of charity on your part?'

'Such conceit!' retorted Lady Emilie. 'Strange as it may seem, it was not my intention to discuss you at all.'

He shrugged, wearing a more humorous expression than Lucy had seen before on his naturally rather austere features, and left the room.

'He is quite right, of course,' said his grandmother, when he was safely out of earshot. 'I have every intention of discussing him. He has, I fear, fallen into deplorably lax ways these last ten years, but I think he should not prove impossible to housetrain, provided you do not set about it in too obvious a manner. However, no doubt you have already begun to discover that for yourself?'

Lucy suddenly recalled her own good manners. 'If you would care to sit down, my lady, I think you may safely do so without clouds of dust arising from the cushions.'

'Thank you.' Lady Emilie seated herself upon the sofa

and surveyed her surroundings. 'Yes, this room is quite presentable, though I must confess I never cared much for Madeleine's taste in furniture. The French style is, to my mind, vastly inferior to that of our own craftsmen. Nothing can hold a candle to Chippendale or Hepplewhite. I cannot now recall what pieces you have in the other rooms. Were they too furnished by Madeleine?'

'I think not,' said Lucy. 'The rest of the furniture is English, but of a very poor quality. I imagine it came from a sale, or perhaps was a gift—'

'From my other grandson,' Lady Emilie concluded, nodding. 'Very likely. He is not ungenerous, Ralph, but I have noticed he rarely gives away anything he values highly himself. This farm, for example, was never particularly productive, even in my husband's day: its sloping fields make the land too difficult to work. Tell me, what did you make of Ralph when you met him?'

Lucy had the impression she was being asked this question for some definite reason, so she replied in guarded tones, 'He was not—uncivil to me . . .'

'That I'll warrant! He has an eye for a pretty face, my dear, so take care! If Letty was less than kind to you, it is perhaps worth remembering that she has good reason to regard with suspicion any other woman below the age of fifty, though I suspect her desire to avoid having them in the house is not so much due to jealousy as to expediency. No,' Lady Emilie mused, half to herself, 'I do not think Letty has been jealous for years where Ralph is concerned, but she cannot abide being made a fool of. I fear you must have come as something of a shock, my dear, for she was under the impression you were both a widow and of middle-age . . .'

'I was married at seventeen, my lady, and widowed only three months later. Since then I have lived with my father and stepmother in London.'

'Hmm! I can well imagine *that* was not a particularly

comfortable arrangement. But surely it is an exaggeration to say you had nowhere to go?'

Lucy knew instinctively that Lady Emilie would be satisfied with nothing less than the truth. Briefly she gave an account of her father's gambling and his subsequent bankruptcy.

The old lady heard her out and then nodded her head. 'And so the poor fellow must languish in prison until his debts are paid. Is there no-one to whom you can turn for financial assistance?'

Lucy sighed. 'I fear most of his friends have come to his rescue so often in the past they have now lost patience with him. Besides, this time it is a substantial sum.'

'Even so, I must confess I am a little bemused by the speed with which you contracted a marriage to my grandson,' said Lady Emilie. 'When I heard the news, frankly I suspected the worst, yet you do not strike me as an adventuress . . .'

'I assure you I am not! But my situation was desperate and your grandson insisted on marriage in order to forestall any gossip—'

'Ha!' snorted Lady Emilie. 'More likely give rise to it!'

'And I was greatly attracted to Brooktye when first I saw it,' Lucy continued truthfully. 'Despite its run-down state I saw its possibilities. What is more, it gives me a chance to live in the country again.'

'If you can persuade my grandson to use the land—or at least sublet it so that it may provide a source of income,' said Lady Emilie sharply, 'then you will earn my unqualified admiration. At present he does nothing but play with his vineyard.'

'I think it means a great deal to him,' said Lucy.

'I've no doubt it does.' The old lady's expression softened somewhat. 'What we have to remember about Philippe is that he has been deprived of everything—

parents, inheritance, even his wife. Not that *she* was any great loss, but nonetheless it has left him very much alone. The vineyard represents his clinging to the past, I fear. Your task, my dear, is to bring him back to the present.'

'I do not think that I—'

'You will! You cannot help it.' Lady Emilie said forcefully. 'Why you married him—or indeed, why he married you—seems to me quite irrelevant. What matters is the future, and having met you I feel more hopeful about it than I have for some time.'

Lucy flushed. 'It is kind of you to say so, my lady.'

'You had better call me Grandmère. Or Grandmama, if that would come more easily to you.'

'I would like to call you Grandmère, if I may.' Lucy leaned forward earnestly. 'I'm afraid I am quite ignorant on the matter of family history. It must have been your daughter who married the Comte de Sevignac?'

Lady Emilie smiled. 'I too am of French descent, as you may have guessed, though I left the country of my birth when I was only fifteen and came to England with my dearest Ninian. Ah, such a man! Eight children we had, though only five survived their infancy. Anne was my eldest daughter, as bold and strong-willed as her father. She had suitors by the score but showed no inclination to marry any of them, so at last in desperation I sent her to visit my cousin Clementine, who was well established at the French court. It was there she met François de Sevignac and decided she would have no other man. I believe she was happy . . .' A cloud passed over Lady Emilie's face. 'So strong and healthy she seemed, with hardly a day's illness in her life, yet she never really recovered from Philippe's birth and died of a fever when he was three months old.'

Lucy's eyes misted over with sympathy, not only for Anne but also for the baby son she had left behind.

'What a terrible thing . . . !'

'Terrible,' Lady Emilie echoed sadly. 'The Comte was heart-broken. He did not remarry but devoted himself instead to his lands and to his King. Losing both was a blow from which he never recovered.'

'But he escaped the Terror—and brought his family here to seek refuge with his wife's relatives?'

'What other choice was open to him? I fear it was never a happy arrangement. When the Comte died Philippe was too proud to accept charity from Ralph—it was only for Madeleine's sake he agreed to lease Brooktye. But it never suited her here. She was desperate to return to France.' The old lady's mouth turned down disapprovingly. 'You have nothing to fear from her memory, my dear. She made little lasting impression upon her husband—or this house.' She glanced round the room. 'There are a few items of furniture at the Dower House I have no further use for, and which I think would be more to your taste. I will have them sent over. What would you like for a wedding present?'

'A teapot,' said Lucy without hesitation, adding with a little smile, 'if you please, Grandmère.'

Lady Emilie rose to her feet. 'Very well, a teapot it shall be.'

Almost as if he had been waiting outside the door M. de Sevignac made a timely appearance, wearing an impassive expression which did not alter when his grandmother tapped him on the shoulder and said, 'You have shown more sense than I gave you credit for. Kindly see me to my carriage.' Turning to Lucy she added softly, 'You may kiss me on the cheek, my dear.'

Lucy did as she was bid. 'Goodbye, Grandmère. And—thank you for coming.'

The old lady said wryly, 'I will put in a good word for you at the Park. But I warn you, Letty is a damned obstinate creature!'

Before following his grandmother from the room M. de Sevignac's eyes rested briefly on Lucy, and in them was an unmistakable glow of approbation. He said nothing, but Lucy watched them depart with a heart grown miraculously lighter.

CHAPTER
FIVE

THE month of June saw many changes at Brooktye Farm. Once the house had been attended to, the larder stocked, hams and sides of bacon salted and hung up to dry, and every room was full of the scent of lavender polish, Lucy turned her attention to the yard outside. Soon it was swept, fresh-smelling and inhabited by a horde of happy hens who expressed their gratitude daily by presenting her with large speckled eggs, firm-shelled and golden-yolked. She had, moreover, cleared the overgrown path to the front door and attempted to impose some discipline on the profusion of rambling roses that surrounded it, so that it might now be entered without fear of having one's hat snatched off by a thorn. She had also discovered, to her delight, the existence of a herb garden at the side of the house, with an abundance of rosemary, thyme, sage and pennyroyal mint.

'There is so much to do it is difficult to know where to begin,' she sighed one evening when they were relaxing after their evening meal, which now took place in the dining-room. It was a time, by common consent, for rest after a day in which all of them had laboured equally hard, and was often spent in total silence, no-one feeling lively enough to make inconsequential chit-chat.

M. de Sevignac looked across the table at his wife. 'I hope you are not overtaxing yourself,' he said, frowning. 'It was never my intention you should take on the rôle of gardener as well. That should be Junot's work.' He glowered at his steward. 'However, I fear he has little aptitude for growing things, and would even snip off the flowers on the vines if I did not watch him constantly.'

Lucy gave Junot a reassuring smile and said quickly, 'I do not believe, Monsieur, you have remarked on the beautiful wedding gift we received from your grandmother. It stands on the side-table.'

He stared at the magnificent silver tea-urn on circular legs, an elegant band of chasing round the top. 'What on odd thing for her to have chosen—'

'Not at all. She knew we had need of one. And she has also sent a mahogany sofa-table and a lovely little escritoire for which she said she had no further use. If you are agreeable I should like to call upon her in a day or so to express our gratitude?'

He nodded and said rather grudgingly, 'It seems you have succeeded in winding my grandmother round your little finger. I congratulate you.'

Lucy glanced quickly at him, but in the dim light it was impossible to make out his expression. Ever since his grandmother's visit his moods had been disconcertingly unpredictable, swinging from moments of near-affability when he was prepared to discuss with her the progress of his vines and listen patiently to her household queries, to moments when he seemed full of unreasonable irritation and would stride impatiently away while she was in mid-sentence. Even Junot had remarked upon it. 'Grandmère has shown me great kindness,' she said quietly. 'I cannot help but be grateful that at least one member of your family should see fit to make me welcome.'

M. de Sevignac's grey eyes gleamed. 'I have no doubt Cousin Ralph would show you even greater kindness, given a little encouragement,' he drawled, 'if that would please you—'

'It would not please me at all,' she retorted, 'as you must very well know. Indeed, I shall be more than content if I never set foot inside Stansgate Park again!'

For a moment he regarded her in silence, his inscrutable gaze resting on her simple gown of blue gingham and the white kerchief around her neck. Then he said casually, 'Nonetheless it is only natural for a woman to hanker after finery and baubles. You may find the temptation too great . . .'

She stared at him in amazement. 'Are you suggesting that if your cousin offered me charity I should accept? Is that what you *want* me to do?'

Angrily he snapped, 'Of course it is not what I want!' Flinging his napkin on to the table, he rose to his feet, pushing back his chair with such force it almost toppled over. 'However, I fear you are only human, Madame, despite all the evidence to the contrary!' He strode from the room, slamming the door behind him.

Embarrassed, Lucy looked down at her plate. Was his last remark intended to be an oblique reference to their wedding night? And why should he taunt her with insinuations about his cousin when she had given him no reason to suspect she found Sir Ralph anything but odious?

'Please not to be upsetted, Madame,' Junot's sympathetic voice broke into her thoughts. 'It is only that Monsieur is sad he cannot buy you pretty things. He knows how you wish for them—'

'But I *don't* wish for them, Junot,' Lucy assured him. 'At least,' she added truthfully, 'I would be glad of a new gown—and perhaps a more fashionable bonnet for going to church—but it is not exactly a hardship to go without either. As for baubles and gee-gaws—why, they don't even suit me particularly!'

Junot fixed her with mournful brown eyes. 'Madame does not desire jewels?'

'Of course not. What use would they be? I could hardly wear them while feeding the hens!'

He grinned happily. 'Too good for the hens,' he agreed and began to clear the table.

Lucy yawned and pressed a hand to her aching back. 'Junot, I am tired. Let us leave the dishes for Mrs Thrupp tomorrow morning, and go early to bed.'

But, as was all too common in the past few weeks, once she was in bed her mind proved far too active for sleep. Perhaps she was unconsciously waiting for the knock on the door that never came, for M. de Sevignac had made no further attempt to assert his rights as a husband, and in some ways the postponement only served to make her more nervous. For postponement she felt convinced it was. Once or twice she had surprised a look in his eyes that made her suddenly breathless, and she had become intensely aware of his physical presence, unable to be at ease when he was in the same room. The atmosphere between them seemed heavy and oppressive, and at times she found herself wishing the storm would break and put an end to this tension.

Restlessly she turned and tried instead to think of William and the few brief memories of their life together; but it seemed like a dream. She tried to conjure up a picture of his frank, open face, the smiling blue eyes, the unruly lock of light brown hair that always fell over his forehead. So young, so heroic in his uniform, so considerate in his lovemaking . . .

She frowned with the effort of trying to remember. William's slender body against hers, his whispered reassurances, the moment of pain she had endured for his sake . . . and the nights spent lying in his arms, waiting for the dawn. How different from the scene that had taken place here, in this room, between herself and M. de Sevignac! Totally lacking William's sensitivity he would have taken her merely to satisfy his own selfish desires, without even a pretence of love. 'Love!' she thought bitterly. 'He has not a morsel of sentiment to spare for anything but his vines. If he does come knocking at the door 'twill be a simple matter of imposing his authority as a husband—and nothing more!'

Angrily she threw back the bed-clothes. The room seemed stifling, the heat of the day still trapped beneath the eaves. She moved to open the window even wider and let in the cool night air, but as she did so her eye was caught by a flicker of light down by the barn, as if someone were walking behind the hedge that divided the garden from the path leading to the vineyard. Could it be M. de Sevignac on the look-out for rabbits, anxious for his vines even at this hour? Yet she was almost certain she had heard him come upstairs to his room some time ago.

But although she watched for a full ten minutes longer she did not see the light again, and eventually dismissed it as a trick of moonlight upon glass. Even so, she returned to bed a little disquieted.

The following morning she drove into Cuckfield with Junot. When they had concluded their business at the butcher's she left Junot flirting quite outrageously with the plumply beguiling widow who ran the bakery and went to call on Mrs Best, who was delighted to see her and full of genuine concern as to how things were going at Brooktye. When Lucy had answered all her questions as truthfully as she might, she responded with one of her own. 'Mrs Best, do you know of a man called Will Voller?'

'Aye, I do.' Mrs Best's lips folded in a tight line. 'He's not been troubling you, I hope?'

'Not exactly. But he has been up to the house . . .'

'Well, that's no surprise!' Mrs Best nodded knowingly. 'Thick as thieves with your Mollie Thrupp, he is.'

'Is he? She made no mention of it.'

'Because she's a sly one, same as he. Two of a kind they are, and neither one of them to be trusted. Better lock up your valuables, m'dear, if *he*'s been snooping around.'

'I don't think we have any valuables.' Lucy was still troubled. 'What does he *do*, exactly? Does he live round here?'

'Of no fixed abode, as they say. As to what he does, he's a beggar, a drunkard, a trickster and a thief and when he's about it usually means trouble for someone. Mr Best!' She called to her husband, who was just passing the door with a heavy barrel of ale. 'Has Will Voller been seen in the town again?'

'He has that, about three weeks ago. Came in here and I refused to serve him, but then he went on asking questions—' He broke off abruptly as his eye fell on Lucy. 'Why? Has he been up to something?'

Questions about what? wondered Lucy. Or whom?

'He's been hanging around Brooktye,' replied Mrs Best. 'Probably taken up with that woman again. You know, 'twouldn't surprise me if he were hiding out in her cottage!'

Mr Best frowned. 'I haven't set eyes on him in the town for a week or two.' He looked at Lucy. 'If he comes again you tell your husband to see him off in no uncertain manner. You don't want him hanging about on your land. I don't like the sound of that—I don't like the sound of that at all!' The expression of anxiety on his face did nothing to ease Lucy's own concern.

Junot emerged from the bakery looking somewhat flushed and carrying a loaf of still-warm bread which he informed Lucy was a gift from Mrs Porter.

'But how kind!' Lucy murmured, straight-faced. 'She seems a most pleasant sort of person—and obviously has a very high regard for *you*, Junot!'

He grinned at her. 'She says all Frenchmen are quite

mad. Myself, I think she does not mind a little madness now and then.'

As they turned into the drive on their way back to Brooktye Lucy asked Junot to point out to her Mollie Thrupp's cottage; and if he had not done so she doubted whether she would have seen it since it was overgrown with ivy and obscured from the gaze of passers-by behind a screen of unclipped yew. She could not detect a flicker of life through the cracked and dirty windows . . . yet *were* they being watched?

'Junot, stop!' she called out peremptorily.

Startled, he reined in the mare and turned to her with an enquiring look.

'There is something I must say to Mollie Thrupp,' she told him, descending from the gig before he had a chance to protest. 'A change of menu for supper . . .'

The gate was off its hinges and the path covered with weeds. She rapped loudly on the door with her knuckles and stepped back to glance at the upper floor. The cottage windows stared back at her like baleful eyes.

After a long wait the door opened cautiously and Mollie's face appeared, blotched with weeping.

'Oh, I am sorry to disturb you,' Lucy began, momentarily disconcerted by the bleak misery on Mollie's sullen face, 'but I have just bought a neck of veal from the butcher in Cuckfield and thought perhaps we might have it roasted tonight . . .'

Mollie gazed at her blankly, as if she had not understood a word, and drew her shawl tighter round her shoulders.

'Are you not well?' Lucy inquired. 'If you would prefer to stay at home for the rest of the day—?'

'No, I'll come,' said Mollie ungraciously. She had now recovered from her initial surprise and her face took on its habitual insolent expression. 'Was that *all* you wanted?'

'Yes—yes, that's all . . .' Lucy tried to steal a sur-reptitious glance over Mrs Thrupp's shoulder into the dark, gloomy room beyond.

'What's amiss?' Mollie demanded. 'Afraid I might have his Lordship hidden away? Is that why you come knocking on my door for no good reason?'

Lucy was almost speechless with indignation. 'Mrs Thrupp!' she gasped. 'How dare you—?'

'Well, you're barking up the wrong tree,' Mollie continued, unrepentant. 'There's no-one here but me.'

Lucy made some attempt to retrieve her dignity. 'I suspected no such thing, I assure you. My sole reason for calling was to—' She broke off as a noisy clatter of saucepans came from inside the cottage.

For a few seconds they stared at each other in silence. Then Mollie said, 'That plaguey cat, always coming down here, bothering me for food.'

Lucy inclined her head coldly, but as she was about to turn away she noticed the woman's shawl had fallen away from her neck, revealing a large purplish bruise, and felt a surge of reluctant sympathy. Plainly Will Voller was a far from easy lodger, if her suspicions were correct. 'Very well, Mrs Thrupp,' she murmured. 'I shall expect you shortly.'

She returned to the gig resolved to speak with M. de Sevignac on the matter. Surely he would not willingly condone the harbouring of such an unsavoury character on his land.

All thoughts of Will Voller, however, fled from her mind when they reached the yard and she saw they had a visitor. Sir Ralph Stansgate, astride a raking grey, was talking to her husband. Both of them turned as the gig drew to a halt beside them and M. de Sevignac stepped forward to assist her descend. 'Our popularity in-creases,' he said in an undertone. 'Cousin Ralph profes-ses a sudden interest in my vineyard, though I suspect that is not the real reason for his visit.'

'No, indeed.' Sir Ralph swung himself out of the saddle with surprising ease for such a heavily built man. 'The real reason has just arrived.' He bowed and raised Lucy's hand to his lips. 'Greetings, fair cousin. I trust Philippe is treating you well?'

'Well enough, thank you,' she replied coolly.

His yellow-green eyes appraised her, making her uncomfortably aware that she was wearing the same travelling-gown as when he had last seen her, on her wedding day. 'A new governess arrives today,' he said, 'and you may depend upon it she will be tediously plain. How I wish it might have been you, Goddess. There are times when my wife is cursed unreasonable.'

'Leave her alone, Ralph.' There was no mistaking the underlying menace in M. de Sevignac's voice.

'My dear Philippe—what sort of villain do you imagine I am?' Sir Ralph inquired mildly. 'You will give Cousin Lucy quite the wrong impression of me. I respect you both and wish you only happiness. God knows you deserve it.' Lucy could have sworn there was almost a ring of sincerity in these last words.

But M. de Sevignac was implacable. 'We do not always get what we deserve, Ralph.'

'That is true.' Sir Ralph tapped his gleaming boot pensively with his whip. Then he straightened. 'Now you have a wife, Philippe, I trust you mean to take your rightful place in local society. Has Letty invited you to our Midsummer Ball?'

'You know very well she has not.'

'That must have been an oversight. You will come, I beg you.'

'We have no intention of coming where we are not invited.'

'But I *am* inviting you, damn it! Am I not master in my own house?'

M. de Sevignac gave a tight smile. 'Whether or not that is the case, I have no wish to expose my wife to insult and ridicule.'

Sir Ralph glanced at Lucy, who was listening to this exchange without undue concern, since she had no doubt that the last thing M. de Sevignac intended was to accept the invitation. It had been a mere whim on Sir Ralph's part, a way of making mischief for both his cousin and his wife. Lucy could well imagine just how angry Lady Stansgate would be if they were to present themselves at the Ball.

'I think that between us we could protect Madame your wife from any insults or ridicule she might receive,' Sir Ralph said lightly. 'At least it would enliven the proceedings, which otherwise promise to be a dead bore. What do you say, Goddess? Are you brave enough to take on all the dragons of the County at one go?'

Before she could utter a word M. de Sevignac said quickly, and to her utter amazement, 'Very well. We will come. But you had best warn Letty first, so that she has time to adjust to the idea.'

Sir Ralph shrugged. 'Where would be the fun in that?' He fixed his cousin with a challenging look. 'Good! And bring some wine with you. We will try it on our guests when they are least expecting it and you will be able to see for yourself what is their reaction.' He swung himself into the saddle. 'Then I shall expect you both on Saturday evening—unless, of course, you turn coward at the last moment!' Turning his horse roughly, he took off down the drive at a swift canter, with scant regard for potholes. M. de Sevignac watched his departure with an enigmatic expression.

'What on earth made you say such a thing?' Lucy turned to her husband, appalled. 'We cannot possibly go to the Ball!'

'I think that now we cannot possibly stay away,' he said grimly.

'But you only accepted out of pique—or pride,' she accused. 'Have you no thought for me? I am the one who will be treated like dirt beneath your cousin Letty's feet!'

He glanced at her horrified face and said, with an air of condescension she found infuriating, 'I thought all women liked going to Balls. Surely you will find it gratifying to be fussed over and pursued by a horde of bucolic admirers?'

'If I am not cut completely dead!' she retorted. 'And there is another consideration. I have nothing to wear.'

He smiled ironically. 'How like a woman! If that is all you are worried about there is a trunk full of gowns and materials somewhere in the attic. Junot will fetch it down for you.'

She stared at him disbelievingly. 'Do you mean clothes that belonged to your first wife?'

He gave a careless shrug. 'Madeleine had more ball-gowns than she could possibly expect to wear, living in the country. Naturally she had to leave them behind when she returned to France. There should be at least one that Letty has never set eyes on, if that is what concerns you. Indeed, I am quite willing to go through them myself and see if I can remember –'

'I positively *refuse* to go to the Ball dressed in your wife's cast-offs!' She glared at him. 'And it is quite unreasonable of you to suggest it. If we *must* go I insist upon having a new gown.'.

He said curtly, 'I am afraid that is out of the question.'

'Are you telling me we cannot afford it?' Now was the moment, perhaps, when she would discover the truth of his situation . . .

'Yes, that is exactly what I am telling you. What few resources I have are needed for more important things than ball-gowns.'

'Such as your wretched vineyard, I suppose?'

'Such as my wretched vineyard,' he agreed. 'Junot!'

Junot, who had all this while been pretending to rub down the mare in the stable, with both ears trained on the conversation taking place in the yard, emerged with a blankly amiable expression on his face. 'Yes, Monsieur?'

'Fetch down that trunk from the attic and help Madame find a ball-gown.'

'Yes, Monsieur!'

Lucy lifted her chin. 'I shall not go.'

For a moment M. de Sevignac looked almost weary. 'That would, of course, be the easy way out for both of us. But we must go, Madame, if we are ever to hold up our heads and kill once and for all the rumours that are circulating about both of us.' He turned abruptly, and strode off in the direction of the barn, leaving Lucy to stare after him.

'You have made a miracle, Madame!' Junot exclaimed, also staring at his master's retreating back.

Lucy looked at him, uncomprehending.

'Always he shuts himself away, never speaking to a person,' Junot explained. 'When at the beginning people try to be friendly he say go away, please. Now he is prepared to fight, to meet the enemy face to face. It is *your* doing, Madame.'

'I don't think so,' Lucy said doubtfully. 'If anything it was his cousin who provoked him into accepting.'

But Junot was carried away with his own enthusiasm. I get down the trunk. Madame—the first Madame, you understand—?' he grimaced, '—had many beautiful clothes. You will see . . .'

And if the first Madame had many beautiful clothes, Lucy reflected, as she followed him slowly into the house, *who* had paid for them? Or had she in fact run up so many bills that she left her husband penniless? Somehow Lucy found it difficult to believe M. de Sevignac had ever been so weakminded as to allow such a thing to happen, even in his youth. Unless, at some early stage of their married life, Madeleine de Sevignac had been able to coax her husband into giving her whatever she wanted.

Prompted more by curiosity than by any hope of finding something suitable to wear, Lucy followed Junot upstairs and held the ladder steady while he mounted to the loft. After some time his perspiring face appeared above her. 'The trunk is too heavy for me to move, Madame. Shall I throw down whatever may be suitable?'

'Do as you please,' she said, a little ungraciously. ''Twill be a wonder if the moths and the mice between them have not already had their pick . . .' But when Junot began to toss down armful after armful of dazzling brocades and velvets, silks and gauzes, she gazed open-mouthed at the mounting pile at her feet. Certainly Madeleine had had expensive tastes! No wonder M. de Sevignac had no money left to indulge his second wife's desire for a single gown.

Junot came down the ladder looking dusty but triumphant. 'There! What do I tell you?'

'The materials are fine enough,' she admitted, 'but the fashions are years out of date.' She held up the train of a gown in silver gauze woven in an intricate butterfly design. 'This is lovely and there are yards of it, but the style is hopeless.'

Junot picked up a simple chemise gown of white muslin, unmistakably French-inspired, with short puffed sleeves.

'Too plain,' Lucy declared. 'Unless . . .' Taking the muslin from him she put the silver gauze against it. 'Unless I make the gauze into an over-tunic . . .'

Junot beamed. 'Madame will look ravishing! She will

be the sensation of the Ball—like Cinderella.'

'Unfortunately there is no fairy godmother to wave her magic wand,' Lucy reminded him. 'And only three days left in which to achieve the transformation.'

Junot dismissed the problem with an airy wave of his hand. 'It can be done. You will leave the cooking to Mollie Thrupp and me . . .'

Lucy looked at him thoughtfully. 'It means much to you that your master should start taking an interest in life outside Brooktye, doesn't it, Junot?'

'Of course!'

'You would like to see him "take his rightful place in society", as his cousin said, and settle down?'

'No!' His emphatic reply startled her.

'No? But I thought—'

'Monsieur cannot be happy in England.' Junot's eyes clouded wistfully. 'One day we shall return to France.'

'Surely that is impossible?'

'Not impossible,' he said, shaking his head. 'Many people already go back.'

'But what of the vineyard—the de Sevignac estate? Was it not divided up and given away?'

Junot's expressive face grew tragic. 'Three years ago, during the Peace, we visit our home. The vines are neglected, the house in ruins. Much work is necessary—but we could do it.' His chin jutted out with uncharacteristic obstinacy. 'Yes, Madame, we *could* do it!'

Lucy found the thought disturbing. 'Yet he has worked so hard to create a vineyard here in England. No, Junot, I believe he will settle here quite happily if he will only make the effort.' She turned her attention to the two gowns. 'And now I had better set to work. Since it seems we must go to the Ball I do not intend to give Sir Ralph Stansgate—or his wife—any reason to criticise my appearance even again!'

CHAPTER
SIX

ON the evening of the Midsummer Ball at Stansgate Park Lucy surveyed herself in the clouded looking-glass in her room and decided that what little she could see pleased her well enough. No-one, she thought, would guess that she was wearing two gowns fashioned together, and both of them ten years old. The neckline, perhaps, looked rather bare, but her little silver locket with a pearl drop was far too simple for the occasion and would only draw attention to the fact she had nothing else. She dressed her hair in a casual style, using ribbons and a white plume from an old bonnet, and descended the stairs with some apprehension, wondering what M. de Sevignac would find to wear. Surely he would not be so insensitive as to stand up before the assembly in his usual fustian!

She was certainly not prepared for the elegantly attired and unquestionably aristocratic stranger who awaited her in the drawing room. For a few moments they stared at each other in mutual surprise.

'Excellently done, Madame,' he said at last. 'Your appearance will cause quite a stir. Cousin Letty may even forget to smile.'

'Thank you, Monsieur,' she said demurely. 'You too are looking exceeding grand.'

He glanced down at his tail-coat and tight-fitting cream pantaloons. 'We must hope a moth does not fly out at some inopportune moment.' His eyes narrowed as he scrutinised her appearance. 'I must confess I do not recall—'

'No, you would not,' she interrupted hastily. 'For it is two gowns made into one, though I would defy even the most critical eye to discern the fact—' She broke off, uncomfortably aware that his gaze was resting on her décolletage, and put up a hand to adjust the thin gauze covering her shoulder.

'Wait here,' said M. de Sevignac, and strode from the room.

By the time he returned Lucy had rearranged the shawl to conceal as much as possible of her neck and shoulders.

'Take it off,' ordered her husband.

Lucy turned to stare at him; and then her eyes fell on the necklace dangling from his fingers.

'The finishing touch,' he announced, watching her face.

For a moment she was speechless, transfixed by the fiery, flashing brilliance of the jewels hanging so carelessly from his fingers. 'Are they—diamonds?' she managed at last.

'Of course they are diamonds! Do you imagine a de Sevignac would festoon his wife with paste? Let me put them on for you.'

Obediently she lowered the shawl, shivering a little as the coldness of the setting touched her skin.

'Unfortunately the clasp is damaged. I must remember to have it repaired.' No doubt because of the faulty catch he took an unconscionable time with the fastening, and she was acutely aware of his warm fingers fumbling at the base of her neck. But his touch seemed impersonal enough, and when he finished he stood back to admire the effect. 'There! What do you think?'

She hesitated. The neckless weighed heavy against her neck and the only question that came to her mind was where on earth had it come from? And were there more . . . ?

'Madame looks like a queen,' said Junot, who had followed his master into the room.

'A countess, at least,' he agreed. 'Which is exactly what she is. I will see if the carriage has arrived . . .'

'Carriage?' Lucy was startled into speech.

'Did I not tell you? Grandmère is sending the chaise for us. You forget we have an ally in the enemy camp.'

'It sounds as if we are going into battle,' Lucy said faintly.

'So we are. Were you not aware of it?' His eyes were gleaming with anticipation. 'I believe I heard the sound of wheels . . .'

When he had gone Lucy turned to Junot and remarked a little tremulously, 'I feel more like Cinderella every moment. How wrong I was to doubt the existence of a fairy godmother! Even the carriage has been conjured out of thin air. But what dreadful thing, I wonder, will happen at midnight?'

Junot grinned with delight. 'Nothing, Madame! It will be a triumph, you will see!'

'I wish I had your confidence. I fear, indeed, we may be routed and forced to retire ignominiously from the field.'

As they swept through the gates leading into the grounds of Stangsgate Park Lucy felt a sinking feeling in the pit of her stomach. 'I hope you will not abandon me completely when we arrive,' she said nervously to her husband, 'and disappear into the card-room for the duration of the evening, as was my father's custom.'

'I have no intention of abandoning you, never fear. Together we shall present a united front, the very picture of marital devotion.'

Chilled by the irony in his voice she fell silent. Lightly she touched the necklace again, as if to convince herself it was real and not merely a figment of her imagination.

'Leave it alone!' His eyes caught the whiteness of her glove as she put her hand to her neck. 'I told you, the catch is faulty. It is best you do not fiddle with it.'

'But what if it should give way—?'

'Such a thing is hardly likely to go unnoticed. In any case I shall be near at hand to keep watch on it, I promise you.'

She sighed and eased her position, at the same time stubbing her toe against an object that seemed to occupy a good deal of the floor space. 'What *is* that?' she inquired a trifle irritably, for her feet were encased in only the lightest of slippers.

'A case of wine for Ralph,' came the brief reply.

Their carriage drew up outside the Palladian frontage of Stansgate Park behind two others, and they were thus able to merge with a little knot of people gathered in the entrance hall, so that their arrival was less noticeable. The moment of truth, however, came when they were announced. A hush fell over the room and eyes turned expectantly towards them. Lucy's fingers tightened on her husband's arm, but she held her head high as he led her towards their hostess.

It was Sir Ralph who stepped forward to greet them first, taking Lucy's hand and raising it to his lips. 'Bravo, Goddess,' he said in an undertone, giving her a look that was boldly admiring. 'Welcome to Stansgate Park—for the second time.'

She acknowledged his salute with as gracious a smile as she could manage, inclining her head towards him before allowing her gaze to travel towards his wife. Lady Stansgate stood immobile, her colour first rising and then receding to leave two bright pink spots on her cheeks.

'Here is a pleasant surprise, my dear,' Sir Ralph was saying loudly, turning to his wife. 'Cousin Philippe and his lovely wife were able to join us after all!'

At his words a confused babble broke out among the guests as the ladies exclaimed in wonderment, laughing behind their fans, and the gentlemen raised their quizzing glasses to inspect Lucy from glowing copper curls to slippered foot, giving particularly close attention to the brilliant gems that surrounded her neck.

Under cover of this upsurge of noise Lady Stansgate's frosty greeting passed almost unnoticed. 'Philippe,' she murmured, looking down with an inscrutable expression at his dark head bowed over her hand. Her eyes moved to Lucy and rested briefly on the necklace. With difficulty she achieved a stiff nod. 'Madame.'

'Don't she look charming, my dear?' persisted Sir Ralph. 'As for Philippe, I have not seen him so respectable for years!'

M. de Sevignac bowed. 'We thought we must come, if only to prove that we have not slipped irrevocably into bucolic ways.' His gaze passed briefly over the guests who still hovered nearby, watching curiously, and he wore a slight, contemptuous smile. 'Beneath the layers of honest dirt we are, as you can see, quite normal.'

There was a ripple of laughter among the ladies, some of whom pretended to turn away but continued to regard him half-fearfully over their fans, as if he were some wild animal, reputed to be tamed but which might at any moment do something unpredictable.

'My children!' Lady Emilie had risen from the throne-like chair where she had been established so that she might have a good view of the proceedings. 'I am delighted you decided to come.'

Lucy greeted her gladly and kissed her on both cheeks. 'Grandmère, it was kind of you to send your carriage.'

'Come, both of you, and sit beside me so that we may talk—preferably without an audience.' The old lady glared at the company, who tittered appreciatively. 'I want to hear all about the wonderful things you have been doing to the house—so much more interesting than all this idle tittle-tattle . . .'

'Before you go, Goddess,' said Sir Ralph, 'I insist that you promise me the first dance.'

Lucy glanced at her husband.

Sir Ralph smiled. 'Surely you will give your consent, Cousin? You cannot expect to keep such beauty entirely to yourself.'

M. de Sevignac gave a tight answering smile and nodded his assent.

'Excellent!' Sir Ralph turned to Lucy with a look of triumph. 'I shall be there to claim you, Cousin, when the music begins.'

'What a performance!' muttered Lady Emilie as soon as they were able to converse in private. 'I vow I do not know where to award the acting honours.'

'I think they must go to Cousin Letty,' said M. de Sevignac. 'She displayed, I thought, an iron control in the face of what must have been a considerable shock.'

Lady Emilie chuckled. 'Iron control maybe; but inside, let me tell you, she was seething fit to burst her stays.' She gave Lucy a shrewd glance. 'That gown becomes you mightily, my dear, but do not pretend to me it is one of Madeleine's. Her taste was never so subtle.' Her eyes slid round to her grandson. 'And it sets off the Bride's Necklace to perfection. It is good to see it again, Philippe. Indeed, I was beginning to wonder what had become of it . . .'

'It is safe enough, as you see,' he said with a bland smile, before his attention was claimed by a stout gentleman who introduced himself as a near neighbour and engaged him in affable conversation.

'I must confess,' Lady Emilie whispered to Lucy behind her fan, 'I am amazed you were able to persuade him to come.'

'It was not my doing,' said Lucy, and proceeded to regale Lady Emilie with an account of how the challenge was issued and accepted.

The old lady listened, her eyes alight with amusement, and when Lucy had finished she observed, 'You know, 'tis an odd thing, but though my grandsons are as different as chalk from cheese and usually at daggers drawn, beneath it all there lies, I think, a certain mutual respect. I believe they almost enjoy their duels of wit, though heaven knows neither has much cause to love the other.' She sighed. 'Ralph is a strange man and can be tiresome but I will acknowledge he is not one to harbour a grudge. Nor, it seems, is Philippe. Perhaps it is because the one doesn't care and the other has no conscience.'

Before Lucy could ask her to explain the band struck up and she was claimed for the first dance by Sir Ralph.

The evening progressed far more agreeably than she had expected, and she found herself approached in the most amiable manner by several ladies, who apologised for not having called to leave cards. 'But we heard such stories!' exclaimed one plump young matron not renowned for her tact. 'I declare you are altogether different from what we were led to believe . . .'

By whom, Lucy had no difficulty in guessing, for she was aware that her hostess's eyes followed her resentfully about the room. Nor could she help noticing that while her own appearance was attracting a good deal of complimentary attention from the men, so also were M. de Sevignac's dark good looks and tall figure drawing many a speculative feminine glance. However, if he were aware of it he gave no sign, but for the most part remained true to his word, never straying far from his wife's side even though they might be engaged in separate-conversations. When it came to the dancing he stood up once with his hostess and propelled her silently around the room, matching her air of disdain with his own polite indifference. For the rest he partnered only Lucy, though when it came to the country dances he pleaded ignorance and stood aside to allow a variety of young men whisk her about the room so energetically that more than once she feared for the safety of her necklace. She was conscious, moreover, that M. de Sevignac hardly took his eyes from her, even when pretending to listen to an anecdote told him by a gentleman in a gold-embroidered waistcoat.

'You seem to have put some spell on Philippe,' Lady Emilie observed at supper. 'I have never seen him so attentive to a woman.'

'Do not be deceived,' smiled Lucy. 'It is not I but the necklace he watches so assiduously. The catch is loose and he is ready to dart forward and retrieve it the instant it falls.'

'Ha!' The old lady gave a bark of laughter. 'Still, at least he has allowed it to see the light of day.'

'Why did you call it the "Bride's Necklace"?' Lucy asked curiously.

'Because it is not in fact part of the de Sevignac inheritance, but is passed down the distaff side. Originally it was a gift to my grandmother by an unknown admirer, allegedly of royal blood, and is by tradition bestowed on the eldest daughter on her wedding day. It was given to my daughter Anne on the occasion of her marriage to François de Sevignac, and now I am delighted that her son has seen fit to give it to you. It has a certain purity, I have always thought, compared with the de Sevignac jewellery, which is almost entirely composed of coloured gems.' Lady Emilie gave a derisive sniff. 'But I have to rely on memory, for we have not set eyes on them since Madeleine's disappearance. For a while I suspected she had absconded with the lot, though seeing the diamonds around your neck tonight makes me doubt that theory. But in that case – where are they? Have *you* seen them?'

Lucy flushed and shook her head. 'There have been rumours, I know, about the fortune he has hidden away . . .'

'And no smoke without fire, so they say!' rapped out the old lady, before bending closer to whisper, 'Take care – here is your gaoler!'

Realising that her husband had come to stand behind her chair Lucy turned the conversation to more mundane topics. But when, later in the evening, she found herself dancing with Sir Ralph for the third time it was plain that he too was intrigued by the necklace.

'It is a very fine piece, set off to perfection by the whiteness of your skin,' he remarked, his gaze lingering on her shoulders with an intimacy Lucy found far from pleasing. 'And gives the lie to all those who said that Madeleine had taken the jewels back to France. But where are the rest?'

Lucy kept her eyes fixed on his cravat. 'I have no idea, Sir Ralph.'

'Cousin, if you must. Ralph would please me better.'

Aware that he was flirting with her partly to annoy her husband, she smiled distantly. 'Very well, *Cousin Ralph.*'

'Come, Lucy—you can be frank with me. *Have* you seen them?'

She opened her eyes wide, pretending she had not followed his conversation.

'I know very well that Madeleine did not take them back to France,' he went on conversationally. 'She was forced to live by her wits from the moment she set foot on French soil and died a pauper.' He saw that Lucy was staring at him and quickly added, in a lighter tone, 'So if she didn't take them they must still be in Philippe's possession – which seems odd because there must have been many occasions during the last few years when he wanted money badly for his vineyard, and you cannot make me believe he would have thought twice about selling the jewels. Unless, of course, he has sold them gradually and this—' he touched the necklace gently—'is all there is left.'

'Perhaps that is the explanation,' Lucy agreed. Anxious to change the subject as quickly as possible she asked, 'Have your children been allowed to watch the proceedings? I do not think I have caught a glimpse of them.'

'Oh, the girls were gawping through the balusters earlier until their new governess despatched them upstairs. I wish you had seen her —a whey-faced creature who certainly need not fear for her virtue in this house!' He grinned wickedly and then said in an off-hand tone, 'As for Ninian, I doubt you would have noticed him even if he had condescended to make an appearance. Most like he is upstairs with his head buried in a book.'

Lucy felt a pang of pity for the boy whose scholarly nature obviously did not please his father.

It was later in the evening that M. de Sevignac's moment of triumph arrived, when Sir Ralph opened up the case of wine he had brought and surreptitiously passed a few bottles among the more discerning of his guests, hoping to surprise them into some statement of its merit. The reaction was immediate.

'What, sir—have you cheated the Excisemen, to say nothing of Boney himself?'

'Like the wedding host at Cana, Sir Ralph, you seem to have saved the best wine till last.'

'Will you reveal the name of your wine-merchant, or is it a closely-guarded secret?'

'No, I will tell you his name if you insist upon it.' Sir Ralph smiled broadly and flung an arm around his cousin's shoulders, for all the world as though they were bosom friends.

Lucy watched the ensuing scene with some apprehension. How would her husband react, she wondered, to Sir Ralph's unexpected championship of his cause? She need not have worried. Before long it became evident that M. de Sevignac was positively basking in the glory with which he was suddenly surrounded, and for a while she lost sight of him entirely as he became the centre of an excited, enthusiastic crowd of wine-tasters who rolled the golden liquid around their tongues, swallowed it and pronounced it fit for loyalty.

'You should send a hog's head down to the Prince at Brighthelmstone,' suggested a grossly overweight squire whose high colour bore witness to the extent of his own cellar. 'He would undoubtedly grant you royal patronage.'

M. de Sevignac looked uncertain. 'My stocks are somewhat limited—'

'Then you must set your prices high.' This from a gentleman who was usually at pains to conceal his merchant background.

'Dammit, I'm tempted to try for myself! Have you cuttings to spare, sire?'

Lucy could not help similing to herself. Despite the finery, the silks and satins, the polite conversation and fiddlers sawing away in a corner draped with tasselled hangings, this was still a country gathering, where people's thoughts were never far from the soil.

They drove home in companionable silence, M. de Sevignac no doubt occupied with his dreams of a flourishing vineyard supplying wine to every corner of England and thereby cocking a snook at Buonaparte himself.

'Well?' Lucy asked at last. 'Can we claim a victory, do you think!'

'Decidedly. It was never in question, from the moment we entered the room.'

'That was the worst moment. If Cousin Letty had chosen to make a scene—'

'But she did not, though I doubt very much if we have heard the last of it.'

'I must confess I shall not feel in the least put out if we are never invited to Stansgate Park again,' she said candidly. 'Your grandmother I love, but your cousins I find far from agreeable.'

After a pause he said, 'It seems I was right in my first impression of you – a woman of sound commonsense.'

She could tell by his voice that he was smiling. 'Of course! But isn't that what you expected of a wife from "good yeoman stock"?'

In the darkness she heard him chuckle. 'I believe you do not intend to let me forget that remark! Can you ever forgive me?'

'Forgive you? I did not take exception to it, I assure you.'

'I did not mean the remark. I meant for insisting we should be married. It was wrong of me, and thoughtless. I had not given proper consideration to your feelings.'

Too surprised to speak, Lucy could only be thankful for the darkness that hid her face.

M. de Sevignac continued, speaking rapidly, 'When I first suggested Junot should find me a wife it was merely in jest. But he took it seriously enough to bring me a daily bulletin of the young ladies he had considered for the position and found wanting for some reason or other. When he brought you to see me—' He stopped.

Lucy's heart was thudding alarmingly, but still she could not say a word.

M. de Sevignac cleared his throat. 'My desire to protect you from gossip was quite genuine. Nonetheless I realise now I should have given you more time. You could have stayed in Cuckfield—'

Lucy leaned towards him and touched his arm. 'You *have* given me time,' she said quietly, 'and for that I am truly grateful. Staying in the town would have gained us nothing. Only by living at Brooktye could I come to know the house—and you . . .'

His hand closed over hers where it rested on his arm. 'And now that you do know me—?'

She realised he was awaiting her answer with some anxiety but found her throat suddenly constricted. At last she said huskily, 'I am content.'

His grip on her hand tightened and for the rest of the journey they sat without speaking, the atmosphere between them heavy with all that was left unsaid.

When she went to dismount from the carriage on reaching Brooktye Lucy found her legs so unsteady she would have fallen had M. de Sevignac not caught her in his arms. He dismissed the coachman and carried her swiftly into the house, kicking the door to behind him. 'There is no need to rouse Junot . . .'

'No, indeed,' she murmured.

He set her down gently but did not release her. 'I do not believe I told you how beautiful you looked this evening?'

Wordlessly she shook her head.

With a stifled exclamation he pulled her close, his lips finding hers unerringly in the dim light, kissing her tentatively at first, as if half-expecting a rebuff. Then, as she stood unresisting in his arms, his mouth became more demanding until with a groan he crushed her to him.

This time she was powerless to protest. Not even the memory of William could give her sufficient resolve to overcome the trembling weakness invading her limbs, turning her bones to liquid. William belonged to the past, to her girlhood . . . Now she was a woman. As M.

de Sevignac's hands slid beneath her shawl, caressing her spine, she surrendered herself completely to the powerful emotions surging through her blood. Her lips parted involuntarily and her arms slid around his neck.

He raised his head to stare down at her, as if unable to believe her response. 'For God's sake, Lucy,' he murmured in a voice thick with desire, 'don't torment me again. If you mean to refuse me tell me now.'

For answer she only wound her arms more tightly round him, pulling his face down to hers. 'Oh, Philippe,' she whispered against his ear, 'How can I refuse the man I love . . . ?'

Triumphantly he swung her off her feet with such force that the shawl slipped from her shoulders to the ground. He buried his face in her neck, greedily moving his lips across her throat towards the thin gauze covering her breasts.

Then, unbelievably, she was free. Thrusting her from him so roughly she almost fell, he seized the lantern and held it high. 'Where is it?' he snapped.

Stunned, she could only stare at him.

'The necklace . . .' he said impatiently. 'It's gone.'

She put her hands up to her throat and found it bare.

'When did you lose it? I could have sworn you were wearing it when we left the Ball . . .'

'Yes, I was.' Her lips felt bruised and she could not think clearly. 'At least, I remember . . . I *think* I remember touching it when I put on my shawl. It must have come undone. Perhaps it has fallen in the yard—'

He dashed out of the door with the lantern, leaving her to follow. She stood by, watching him helplessly as he searched the cobbles, her hands still clasped around her neck as if unable to believe the necklace was no longer there.

'There's no sign of it,' he said at last. 'Yet I'm certain

this is where the carriage stopped. It must be somewhere . . .'

'It may have fallen off inside the carriage,' she suggested. 'Perhaps it is lying on the floor.'

'That's possible.' He straightened. 'I wonder how far
they have gone.'

'You cannot go after them now! If the coachman finds
it on the floor he will take it to your grandmother—'

'Do you seriously expect any coachman to be stricken
by conscience when he is presented with a necklace of
diamonds? Have you no idea how much that necklace is
worth? I fear you have a rosy view of human nature!'

She winced at the harshness of his words. 'Most
probably he won't even find it tonight, in the dark. If you
go over to the Dower House first thing in the morning—'

'It will be too late!' He thrust the lantern towards her.
'Hold this for me while I saddle the mare.'

Realising it was useless to argue she stood by as he
slipped a bridle over the reluctant mare's head. 'Philippe, I'm sorry—'

'There's no need to blame yourself,' he said curtly. 'It
was my fault for letting you wear it. I knew the catch was
faulty. I should have seen to it long ago.'

So it *was* all that was left, she reflected miserably. The
last valuable piece of jewellery in his possession and she
had been the cause of its loss . . .

He tightened the saddle girth and opened the stable
door. 'Don't wait up for me. I intend to go on searching
till I find that damned necklace!' He kicked the mare
into ungainly action.

She watched him disappear into the darkness, and
then turned sadly back into the house.

As she entered the kitchen she saw a shadowy figure
standing by the table. 'Oh, Junot,' she sighed. 'The most
dreadful thing has happened. You must help me look—'

She stopped abruptly. The man who stepped forward

from the shadows was not Junot.

'Is this what you're looking for?' asked Will Voller.

From his fingers, flashing fire in the lamplight, hung the Bride's Necklace.

CHAPTER
SEVEN

BUT it was not the necklace at which Lucy was staring as if hypnotised. The man before her—gaunt-faced and hollow-eyed, with several days' growth of stubble on his chin—looked too solid to be a ghost, yet there was something about him . . .

Will Voller took the lantern from her nerveless fingers and held it up to illumine his face. Then he smiled—a faintly derisive, one-sided smile that was shatteringly familiar.

'Will—iam?' she said hesitantly, on a note of interrogation.

'So you *do* recognise me? I was beginning to think you never would.' William Forster set the lantern down on the table. 'How are you, Lucy, after all these years? Or perhaps I need not ask . . .' He dangled the necklace before her bemused gaze. 'It seems you've done well for yourself since we last met.'

Lucy swayed and caught hold of the chairback. 'But I don't understand . . . they told me you were dead!'

He shrugged. 'One of those unfortunate muddles at the War Office, no doubt.'

'They came to see me. They said you had been killed when General Abercrombie's troops retreated to the Zype Canal—'

'Left for dead on the battlefield,' he concluded lightly. 'But I made a miraculous recovery, as you can see—like your father.'

She felt as though she were floundering in a dark

tunnel. Here was William—her beloved William—and yet he seemed like a stranger. His features were unchanged, but the blue eyes once capable of such tenderness held a wary, cynical look and the well-shaped mouth was twisted in a bitter line. Moreover, his appearance, over which he had once taken such care, now presented a sorry sight. He looked as though he slept rough and was forced to scavenge for food. Life had treated him harshly, that was evident. 'Oh, William,' she said, her eyes filling with tears. 'What happened—were you taken prisoner?'

'Of course not. I escaped.' He sounded almost boastful.

She tried to collect her scattered thoughts, to make sense of this impossible tangle. 'Then *why* did you not come to find me?'

'I did, when I finally returned to England. I was told you had gone to London.'

'So that is how you knew my father had recovered from his illness . . . But why did you not make some effort to discover our address? Anyone in the village would have given it to you.'

He chewed his lip, as if undecided how to reply.

'Did you not *want* to find me?' she asked incredulously. 'But why should—?' A suspicion took shape in her mind, almost too preposterous to voice. 'Surely it was not because my circumstances had changed—and that I was no longer my father's heir?'

William gave her a look that was frankly resentful. 'You have to admit he wasted no time, producing a son only a scant eight months after the wedding! He must have regained his strength with miraculous speed . . .'

Lucy flushed. 'That was uncalled for—'

'Oh, come, my dear! You cannot pretend still to be the little prude I married. My God, what an innocent you were! I hardly dared touch you for fear I frightened

MARRIAGE OF STRANGERS 103

you to death.' Casually he appraised her bare neck and shoulders, revealed by the low décolletage of her gown. 'How could I have guessed you would grow into such a beauty?'

Her legs were trembling so much they would no longer support her. Groping for the chair, she sat down. 'I cannot believe it! Are you seriously saying you only married me because you thought I would inherit my father's estate?'

'Of course. Cheated of my own inheritance by a brother born a mere half-hour earlier than myself, what else could I do but find a wife with expectations?'

'I thought you loved me—'

'So I did. You were a fetching little thing, though I prefer you as you are now. I could hardly believe my eyes when I saw you that day in Cuckfield, yet I knew at once I was not mistaken. That hair—' He took a step towards her and instinctively she shrank back against the chair. He laughed. 'Perhaps I should have come to look for you, after all.'

'We were *married*, William! I was your wife—' Only now did the full significance of the situation dawn upon her. Her eyes grew wide with horror. 'I am *still* your wife!'

He smiled. 'I suppose you are. In that case you must show me a little wifely consideration. Over this jewellery, for example.' He held the necklace towards the light. ''Tis a pretty thing, and worth a few hundred guineas, I daresay. But where's the rest of the stuff? Surely you must have learned something by now . . .'

Bewildered, she shook her head. 'There is nothing else. Forget the necklace, William—we have more important things to discuss—'

'Believe me, nothing is more important than money when you have none! Indeed, I thought your husband— your *new* husband, I should say—was exceedingly upset by its disappearance. It was his fault, of course, that it fell off with your shawl. Had he not been making love to you quite so passionately it would never have happened.'

'You were watching us?'

He nodded. 'From the passageway. Your return caught me a little by surprise.'

Her mind went to Junot. Why had he not appeared to help her, roused by the sound of their voices? Dear God, surely William had not—? She rose to her feet and stood facing him across the table, her face pale. 'What have you done to our steward?'

'You'll find him snoring safely upstairs. Mollie slipped a draught into his cup of chocolate to ensure he slept soundly while I searched the house.'

'So Mollie Thrupp is your accomplice?'

'She does as I tell her.' he smirked. 'She has a certain fondness for me, I believe.'

'What were you hoping to find?' A sudden pang of remorse struck her. 'Are you hungry? Were you looking for food?'

'Food? No, Mollie keeps me well enough supplied, though I daresay much of it comes from your larder.'

'Then what—?'

'I told you, the rest of the jewels. Rumour has it they're still in this house.'

'That is sheer fiction!' Colour returned swiftly to her face. ''Tis nothing but a story put about by local people. I can assure you the necklace is all M. de Sevignac has left—so you will please give it back to me immediately!'

He ignored her outstretched hand. 'I think not.'

'You cannot possibly mean to keep it!'

He quirked an eyebrow. 'Such outraged virtue! Of course I mean to keep it.'

'But *I* know that you have it. I have only to tell M. de Sevignac—'

'Only you will not.'

She stared at him. 'You sound very sure.'

'Naturally. I intend to use this—' He jangled the necklace—'to buy your silence.'

Lucy frowned, her thoughts racing. 'William, what exactly is it you want me to do?'

'I want your help in finding the de Sevignac jewels.'

'But they don't even exist!'

He went on, 'And I want you to keep quiet. No-one must know who I am.'

She said firmly, 'I shall have to tell M. de Sevignac the truth. Can you not see I am living a lie? He must be told I am not his wife . . .' She faltered.

'What difficulties virtuous women make for themselves! It is not my intention to upset your domestic arrangements, I promise you. If you like being married to the Frenchman—and by your behaviour tonight it seems obvious that you do—then you can rest assured I shall not interfere. Surely it will suit us both to keep quiet about our previous . . . entanglement?'

'Entanglement!' she echoed disbelievingly. 'Legally we are still man and wife, William, and yet you can suggest in all seriousness that we go on as if nothing has happened. No, 'tis quite impossible. I must tell M. de Sevignac everything.' She felt quite faint at the prospect.

'I am afraid I cannot allow you to do that,' he said in a voice grown menacingly quiet. 'Do you not understand, wife, that I am a desperate man? Desperate men resort to desperate measures when they are in danger of losing their freedom.'

She gazed at him, fascinated. 'But why should you lose your freedom? If you will not return the necklace to me now I give you my word I will say nothing about it, not even to M. de Sevignac. Though I must, of course, tell him that we were married—that you deserted me . . .'

'Unfortunately it was not only you that I deserted.' He smiled wryly.

'What do you mean?'

'Must I spell it out for you? I am a wanted man, Lucy . . . a deserter from the Army. Why else do you think I live as I do, forced to beg for food and take shelter where it's offered, no matter how low or how verminous the company I keep? Yet what choice do I have? I cannot return openly to my own home or even put my real name to any piece of paper for fear someone will find me out.'

'Oh, William . . .' She regarded him helplessly, at last beginning to comprehend the gravity of his situation. 'Is that why you call yourself Voller?'

'I exchanged paper with the corpse lying next to me on the battlefield and put a few of my belongings on his person so that I would be reported as dead.'

She nodded. 'Yes, they brought them to me.'

His face grew dark with bitterness. 'You cannot imagine what it was like out there. A man has a duty to save his own skin, to escape if he can find a way out of the mess. That's what war is—a mess! Half the time you don't even know whether you are winning or losing.'

Was it the war, she wondered, that had altered him so? Or had she been too infatuated as a girl to see him in his true colours?

He watched the changing expression on her face and said softly, 'I *should* have come after you. You might have made me forget. Will you help me, Lucy, for old times' sake?'

She said cautiously, 'I will, if I can . . . But if you are so anxious not to be discovered why do you return here, to Sussex? Is there not a danger someone will recognise you?'

A nerve pulsed in his jaw. 'I came to see my brother. He gives me money, on condition that I stay away. But it is never enough.' He held up the necklace again, as if to remind her it was still in his possession. 'I need more, much more. Enough to go north and buy myself some land. There I can make a fresh start—and prove I am after all no less a man than my brother . . .'

Lucy saw the jealousy in his face and was filled with compassion. How he must resent his twin brother, she thought, who by a mere accident of birth had inherited all William most desired. 'But the Bride's Necklace, William, will never buy you land—'

He tossed it contemptuously onto the table. 'Of course it will not. I need the rest.'

She stared at the glittering gems, longing to put a hand towards them, but not daring to make a move. 'What can I say to make you believe there *is* nothing else—?'

He caught hold of her wrist, gripping it so tightly she almost cried out. 'The servant boasts there is more—'

'Junot? That is impossible . . .'

'I have heard him with my own ears. In his cups he talks of a fortune that will one day take his master back to France.'

'That is mere wishful thinking. Junot has never settled in England and dreams that one day they will return to their own home, but M. de Sevignac has no wish to return. He is quite happy here, with his vineyard.'

Abruptly he released her wrist. 'I don't believe you.' For a few moments he paced rapidly up and down the kitchen. When he turned to face her his expression was wary. 'If you honestly believe the jewels do not exist, then you can have no objection to my searching the house?'

She swallowed painfully. 'If it will convince you—no, I have no objection. But if Mollie Thrupp is your accomplice why have you not asked *her* to search the house. Surely she could have done so at any time? Why wait until now?'

'Mollie has her uses, but she is stupid,' he said tersely.

'Do you imagine I would confide in her what I have learned? Or trust her to do the job for me? No, I shall not be satisfied until I have carried out a proper search myself—and I do not mean *now*, by candlelight and with your husband likely to return at any minute. I want to inspect every nook and cranny in this house by daylight. Will you help me?'

She hesitated.

'If you do,' he continued, 'I will undertake to return the necklace.'

'Return the necklace? But why—?'

'Let us call it an investment. It is the price I am prepared to pay for your silence . . . and your help.'

Her eyes were drawn again to the circlet of diamonds lying on the table. Had he underestimated their value? 'What if you don't find the de Sevignac jewels?'

'That is a risk I—and you—will have to take.'

She raised her eyes to his. 'I will help you search the house.'

'And promise to keep quiet about my presence here?'

'I will say nothing until you have safely left the district.'

'Excellent!' His face glowed with triumph. 'Tomorrow?'

'If it can be arranged. We shall have to wait until both M. de Sevignac and Junot are out of the house.'

He nodded. 'Very well.' Scooping up the necklace he thrust it into the pocket of his ill-fitting jacket. 'Until tomorrow, then. You know where you can find me. Mollie will bring any messages.'

She nodded wordlessly.

He stepped closer, taking hold of her chin to turn her face towards the light. 'I warn you, Lucy, if you betray me it will be the worse for you—*and* your Frenchman.' He kissed her hard on the lips, then stepped back to regard her intently. 'Remember, you are still my wife.

Your first loyalty is to me, not your lover. *Au revoir* . . .'
He disappeared into the darkness, silently closing the
door behind him.

Lucy wiped the back of her hand across her mouth, as
if trying to erase the touch of his lips. She felt soiled,
degraded. In such a short space of time William had
destroyed everything she valued, turning her into a liar
and a cheat, a woman with no choice but to deceive the
man she loved.

For she was quite certain now that she loved M. de
Sevignac. William's shadow no longer stood between
them. The romantic young soldier of beloved memory
was revealed as nothing but a childish fantasy. He had
not even cared for her particularly. His lovemaking had
been a means to an end, his tenderness little more than
expediency for fear he 'frighten her to death'. How
innocent she must have been! Yet her father had known
and tried to save her from a foolish marriage. *'Thank
heaven you did not have children . . .'*

She began to shake uncontrollably, in the grip of a
nightmare from which she could see no escape. *She was
still married to William!* Nothing she could say or do
would alter that fact. The contract between herself and
M. de Sevignac was illegal, meaningless . . . How he
would despise her . . .

Supposing she told him the truth? Could they not
between them outwit William? But if it came to a
confrontation she feared William might prove the more
ruthless fighter, since he had more to lose. Admittedly
M. de Sevignac might be distressed at the loss of the
necklace, but for William it was a question of freedom.
She felt certain he would stop at nothing to save his own
neck—not even murder . . .

Briefly she closed her eyes. That was a thought too
terrible to contemplate.

And would M. de Sevignac, she wondered, be equally

distressed by the loss of his wife? She recalled the moment when he held her in his arms, just before he discovered the necklace was missing. Surely then he had come close to confessing the depth of his own feelings—or was she once again in danger of deluding herself? Perhaps she meant no more to him than Mollie Thrupp, merely a convenient outlet for his animal passions. Certainly he had left her without a qualm to go in search of the necklace. Would a man in love have behaved in so cavalier a fashion?

She was being unreasonable. The Bride's Necklace meant so much to him, it was only natural he should be distracted by its disappearance. If only she could win it back, surely that must help to vindicate her in his sight? It would at least prove to him where her true loyalties lay, whatever William had said. Together they would find some way out of this mess, some hope for the future . . .

She straightened her back, suddenly filled with resolve. The sooner she gave William a chance to search the house the better. Then he would satisfy himself that the jewels were not hidden at Brooktye and leave.

But what if he refused to keep his part of the bargain and give back the Bride's Necklace? After all, his inevitable disappointment in discovering that the de Sevignac jewels did not exist might easily make him decide to keep what he already had. No, she would have to think of some cunning scheme to make him return the necklace *before* she helped him search the house.

She put up a hand to her aching forehead, overcome with weariness. In the morning . . . she would think of something in the morning, when her head was clear and she had recovered from the shock of William's reappearance. Soon M. de Sevignac would be returning from his wild-goose chase. She could not face him tonight, that much was certain.

Lighting herself upstairs with a candle, she went to her room and closed the door.

Some time later she heard M. de Sevignac return. When his footsteps sounded in the passage she held her breath, keeping her eyes tightly shut.

The door opened and she sensed that he had come to stand beside the bed. It took all her self control to breathe evenly, in and out, as though she were fast asleep. When his hand touched her shoulder a shock ran through her body but she attempted to conceal it by burying her head more deeply in the pillow with an incoherent murmur.

He swore softly under his breath, then turned on his heel and left the room.

As the door closed behind him she released her breath in a long shuddering sigh. With all her heart she longed to fling it open and call him back, but she could not. *He was not her husband* . . .

If only William were truly dead! The vehemence of her own feelings shocked her as she clenched her fist and pounded the pillow in angry frustration. But the truth was inescapable and could not be battered into whatever shape she desired. With William alive there was no future for her at Brooktye.

Weeping, she fell across the bed and tried to stifle her sobs in the pillow.

CHAPTER
EIGHT

AFTER a troubled night Lucy awoke resolved to say nothing to M. de Sevignac for the time being, but instead try to behave as naturally as possible, though this would be far from easy. That he would have to be told the truth was inescapable; but not until William was safely out of the way.

She found Junot in the kitchen, nursing a sore head. 'I slept—*mon Dieu*, how I slept!' he complained. 'I did not hear the carriage return, Madame . . .'

Across the room Lucy's eyes met those of Mollie Thrupp, maliciously amused. She looked away hastily, feeling like a conspirator.

'And just when my master have need of me,' he groaned. 'He go after the necklace—'

'You must not reproach yourself, Junot,' she said quickly. 'There is nothing you could have done.'

'My master has not slept. At six o'clock he is at work in the vineyard.' He made an effort to rise from his chair. 'I must feed the hens—'

'Leave the hens to me, Junot. Stay here and rest till your head is clearer.' She hurried from the kitchen, picking up the sack of chicken meal on the way.

Once out in the yard she became wary, half-expecting William to appear at any minute, and when footsteps sounded behind her she jumped visibly.

'I am sorry. I did not mean to startle you.' M. de Sevignac's weary eyes searched her face.

With an effort she regained her composure and said

conversationally, 'You rose early. Junot says you have been working since six.'

'I could not sleep.' He frowned, then added, 'You do not inquire whether or not I found the necklace . . .'

Too late she realised her mistake. She should have displayed more anxiety, a wifely concern . . . Dear God, deception did not come naturally to her. What pitfalls lay ahead if she did not take care! Hastily she said, 'Junot intimated that your journey proved fruitless. I am sorry.'

'My grandmother's groom said he had found nothing on the floor of the carriage and I believe he was telling the truth. When I returned I looked again in the yard and in the kitchen where we—we were standing. It seems to have vanished into thin air.'

The constraint between them was almost unbearable. Nervously she said again, 'I am so sorry. If I had taken more care—'

'It was no-one's fault but my own. I should never have let you wear it knowing that the catch was damaged. Heaven knows I could ill afford to lose it!'

Curiosity overcame her diffidence. 'So there really is—nothing else? Those stories are untrue?'

He shrugged. 'I do not even know how they began. Perhaps because at first we seemed to be rich. Madeleine was always extravagant. I could not stop her selling her own jewels, but once she had the money she went mad, buying clothes, furnishing the house—I believe it was a desperate attempt to forget her homesickness. She loved France and hated England. When her brother Armand arrived the situation grew much worse. They never stopped talking of when they could return and how they would disguise themselves in order to survive. It was like a game to them. No-one else took it seriously. Then one night they slipped away—' He stopped.

Lucy waited, her eyes fixed on his face. He was telling the truth, she felt certain of it.

At length he went on, 'I have never admitted to anyone, not even my grandmother, what I am going to tell you now, but as my wife it is your right to know.' If he noticed the look of pain that passed over her face he gave no sign. 'The night they left we had dined with Ralph and Letty at Stansgate Park. She was wearing the Bride's Necklace. When we came back to Brooktye we had a blazing row and she threatened openly to leave me. As she turned to go I seized hold of the necklace and pulled it from her neck by force. That is when the catch was damaged.'

'And that was the night she left Brooktye?'

'She and Armand were gone by morning—and with them the de Sevignac jewels. I suppose it was her way of taking revenge.'

'*Madeleine* took the jewels?'

He nodded. 'You are the only person, apart from myself, who knows it for certain, though I daresay several people suspect the truth. My grandmother certainly does—and Ralph . . .'

'No, he—' She pulled herself up just in time, realising she must not reveal that she had already discussed the matter with Ralph, who was of the opinion Madeleine had died in poverty. Either Ralph must have been mistaken, or else Madeleine had sold the jewels and spent the money, leaving herself with nothing by the time she died.

He was looking puzzled. 'You don't believe me?'

'Of course I do! I never for one instant thought the jewels were still in your possession.'

He stared at her in silence for a moment, then said, 'My dear, I—'

In her anxiety to forestall whatever he was about to say, she uttered the first words that came into her head. 'Will you not show me your vineyard? I fear I am quite ignorant about wine and how it is produced.'

'Certainly I will show you.' He looked surprised but pleased. 'I had not thought you would be interested.'

Feeling as though she were treading a knife-edge, she picked up her skirts and began to cross the cobbles to the gate, saying over her shoulder, 'This must be so different from the vineyards you left behind in France. Is it very much smaller?'

He followed her, diverted at once by the subject so dear to his heart. 'This is about twelve cartonnats—what you would call four acres in England. 'Tis large enough, believe me, when the time comes to spread netting over the top to protect the fruit from the birds.'

'Netting? But it must take yards! Where do you get it from?'

'For years now Junot has been going down to the coast and buying up as much mackerel netting from the fisherman as we can afford. The birds are our worst enemies, next to the rabbits. And mildew, of course.' They had stopped, looking across the rows of sturdy vines. 'What we need now is plenty of sun and only enough rain to keep the ground watered.'

''Tis a wonderful sight,' Lucy murmured. 'I suppose that when you were in France you had little to do with the actual tending of the grapes?'

'That is true,' he admitted. 'Although even as a child I used to find the process quite fascinating.'

She glanced at him, thinking she detected more than a hint of wistfulness. 'Would you go back to France, if you could?'

His face grew bitter. 'The château was partly destroyed and the lands parcelled up and handed over to the peasants. What is there to go back to?' He turned to her, full of compunction. 'I am sorry, I did not mean to speak so harshly. Of course I miss France and would return tomorrow if I thought there was a future for me there, but it would cost a fortune to restore the estate to anything like its former glory. I refuse to be like Madeleine, for ever crying over what I cannot have, like a spoilt child. No, I am content enough with Brooktye.'

She began to walk back down the path, saying lightly, 'And where do you tread the grapes? Shall I be required to help you do so when it is time for the harvest?' Even as she spoke she realised her words were hollow: by October she would be banished from Brooktye for ever.

He smiled. 'We shall need all the hands we can muster at harvest-time, but your feet I think we can do without!' He guided her into the barn.

Once inside Lucy looked about her in amazement. Here were no signs of neglect, but an orderly arrangement of wooden tables, hog's heads, a wine press and empty casks cooped with iron.

'When we pick the grapes we bring them here for vinification,' he explained. 'They go into the press a few hours after picking and the first running comes from the weight of the bunches upon each other. Then we apply a little force and the juice is run into the hog's heads. You can hear fermentation begin almost at once.'

'How long does it take?'

'First we rack it off into clean hog's heads and then leave them all winter. I inspect them in March and if they're not quite fine enough I fine them down still further with fish glue.'

She wrinkled her nose in distaste. 'Fish glue?'

'Don't look so horrified—it is the custom. By the end of March it is all bottled and ready for storing.'

She looked about her. 'But where? I see no bottles.'

'No, because they must be stored in a cool place. Now, where is my *cave*—that is what you are wondering?' He grinned like a small boy with a secret. 'At Brooktye the cellars are damp and derelict, not at all a fit place for my wine. So, where is the coolest place.'

Although she had already guessed she shook her

head, not wanting to deprive him of the pleasure of telling her.

'Come.' He took hold of her arm. 'I will show you my *cave*.'

She allowed him to lead her through the kitchen, where their progress was watched by Junot and Mollie Thrupp, down the passage and into the dairy, a hexagonal room that struck chill even on this warm June day.

'Last year was a good harvest,' he said proudly. 'Six barrels of wine. This year the vines are even stronger and if the weather is good we should fill seven or eight barrels.'

'Then why do you not—?' She hesitated to finish the question.

He read her thoughts. 'Perhaps at first I was afraid that people might accuse me of trying to sell them champagne under false pretences. But now Tom Best, at the Talbot, has found me a merchant who will pay fifty guineas a hog's head.'

'That's wonderful! So Brooktye will soon be supplying the best tables in the land. Why do you not do as someone suggested last evening and send some to the Prince at Brighthelmstone?'

He turned her round to face him, putting a hand on either side of her waist. 'The first day you came, when we stood in the drawing room, I watched your face as we looked out at the vineyard and realised that by some miracle you were the one woman in the world who could understand.' He tilted her chin. 'Thank heaven I found you, Lucy . . .'

The pressure of his lips was light but she stood rigid, willing herself not to respond. The chill she felt had nothing to do with the temperature in the dairy.

He raised his head to stare down at her. 'What is the matter?'

'It is so cold in here,' she said with a little shiver,

turning towards the door. 'Can we not—'

He caught hold of her wrist, swinging her round so that she was forced to meet his eyes. 'You are angry with me. Why? Because of last night?'

Incapable of replying, she tried to pull away but his grip tightened.

'You think I should not have gone after the necklace . . . that I should have stayed with you.' His voice was hard but Lucy could detect an underlying note of pain and self-reproach. 'Perhaps you are right. I thought only of our future. That necklace was the sole insurance we had against some kind of financial disaster—a bad harvest, for example. Can you not try to understand?'

She saw that he had unwittingly provided her with a logical excuse for her behaviour. Better he should think her capable of feminine pique than suspect the real reason for her change of attitude. She made her tone a little petulant. 'I understand all too well! Obviously the necklace means far more to you than I—'

'That is not true, as well you know!' He spoke angrily; then made an effort to moderate his tone. 'If I have hurt your feelings I am sorry. It was quite unintentional, I assure you. Tell me what I can do to make amends.'

Lucy made another attempt to free herself from his grasp. 'You can begin by leaving me alone!' she retorted.

He released her wrist as if it were a live coal. 'Are you serious? Or is this some new game we play?' he asked incredulously.

'I am perfectly serious.' She stood, rubbing her wrist.

'By God!' he exclaimed, exasperated. 'I never knew a woman blow so hot and cold . . .'

She turned away, afraid he would read her face. 'Is it any wonder I am cold, when you keep me talking in this place. 'Tis like a morgue in here.'

Without giving him a chance to protest she marched

along the passage, conscious of an overwhelming desire to escape. She must get away from Brooktye, if only for an hour or so.

'Junot, will you drive me into Cuckfield,' she said as she entered the kitchen. 'There are some groceries we need and a few things from the haberdashers.'

Junot looked up, his brain still befuddled. 'Now? Madame wishes to go *now* . . . ?'

'Yes, at once.' She caught Mollie Thrupp's dark eyes watching her, brimming with curiosity. 'I will fetch my shawl.'

When she had spent as long as she reasonably could wandering about the town she went to find Junot, who was passing the time of day at the Talbot Inn. Tom Best greeted her with the news that the mail coach had brought her a letter. Glancing at the envelope, she recognised Kitty's spidery handwriting and put it away in her reticule to read later.

'I will tell Junot you wish to go home,' said Mr Best. 'He has just taken a hand in a game of cards—'

'Then please do not disturb him,' Lucy said, making a swift decision. 'I will take the gig and drive myself on to the Dower House. There is something I wish to ask of Lady Emilie.'

Tom Best nodded. 'You've found favour with the old Lady, I hear, for all she's a hard one to please?'

'I believe she likes me,' Lucy replied. 'I hope so, for I value her good opinion highly. Tell Junot I shall be back within the hour.'

She found the old lady ill-prepared for visitors, being still abed, but nonetheless pleased to see her.

''Tis the ache in my bones,' she explained, pulling herself up to a sitting position with difficulty. 'Some days it affects me worse than others and I am unable to move about freely till after noon.'

Lucy expressed her sympathy and sat on a chair beside the bed.

'Once upon a time I would not have found a Ball so exhausting,' Lady Emilie sighed. 'Then I would have danced till dawn and gone riding after breakfast. Oh, to be young again . . .' She peered closely into Lucy's face. 'But *you* have no right to be looking so pale! What's amiss? Are you breeding, by any chance?'

Lucy flushed. 'No! No, I am not, Grandmère.'

'A pity. 'Twould give Philippe something else to think about if he had a son. Make him forget the hurt done to him by Madeleine. You know, of course, that she was pregnant when she returned to France?'

Lucy was startled. 'No, I did not know—'

'Well, I doubt it was Philippe's. She had many lovers—including Ralph, if my suspicions are correct.'

'But what happened to the child?'

'It died. Sickly when it was born, so I am told. Survived for only three weeks—and no wonder, in those conditions!'

Lucy said tentatively, 'Then you must know what happened to Madeleine when she returned to France? Did she write letters?'

'She wrote to Ralph. Whether or not she wrote to Philippe I cannot be sure. She remained very bitter towards him till the end, though *why* I've never really understood. I believe he tried to be a good husband to her, but it was an impossible match. Perhaps it might have succeeded in France where they could lead their separate lives and only meet on formal occasions; but here in England, in less ordered circumstances, they proved quite incompatible.' Lady Emilie fixed her with an intent look. 'Never make the mistake, my dear, of thinking Philippe is incapable of strong feeling. He cares far more deeply than he shows.' When Lucy remained silent she put out a bony finger and lifted her chin. 'And I think he cares for you. Promise me that you, at least, will do nothing to hurt him.'

'I promise,' murmured Lucy, feeling suddenly sick.

'There *is* something amiss,' said the old lady astutely. 'Come, you may as well tell me what it is. I suspect you had not called merely to inquire after my health.'

Lucy hesitated. 'Then you do not know—?'

'Know what? For pity's sake, I am not endowed with second sight!'

'The Bride's Necklace . . . Last night I—I lost it.'

'Lost it? How?'

'When we returned home, we—I discovered it had gone. The catch was faulty . . .' Lucy was choosing her words with care. She had no wish to lie to Lady Emilie. 'M. de Sevignac rode after your coachman, hoping perhaps it had fallen on the floor of the carriage, but he—he did not find it.'

'So *that* was the commotion I heard after retiring to bed! But why has none of my household informed me of this?' the old lady demanded.

'He may have asked them not to do so, for fear it would upset you—'

'Upset? Naturally I am upset! The Bride's Necklace meant much to me—and no doubt to Philippe also.'

Lucy was beginning to wish she had kept silent. To her horror she felt tears coming into her eyes and tried to blink them away.

Lady Emilie's sharp eyes missed nothing. 'Does he blame *you*—is that the problem?'

'Not exactly . . . but I do not know what to do. It was all he had left—'

'Ah, so he has admitted it!'

'He said it was his insurance against the future, in case of a bad harvest—'

'My dear child, if that is what worries you, put it out of your mind. I am not quite a pauper and can provide all the insurance that may be needed. Oh, I know he is proud as a peacock but he must learn to be prudent now he has a wife—and perhaps soon a family as well.' The old lady's face softened as she put out a hand to touch Lucy's cheek. 'So there is no need for you to worry on that score. As for the necklace, it will be found, I am sure. Perhaps the servants have already discovered it in a corner of the ballroom, where it fell when you were dancing. After all, it was not your fault if the catch was loose.'

Lucy did not trust herself to speak. She merely held Lady Emilie's hand against her cheek and nodded silently.

As she drove back along the drive from the Dower House her mind was so busy with this new revelation about Madeleine that she almost ran down the youth who came walking round the corner towards her, apparently also lost in thought. He had looped over his arm the reins of a grey horse, which threw up its head so violently on encountering the gig that the boy was pulled of balance and fell to the ground.

Lucy reined in the mare and turned at once to look at him. 'Are you hurt?'

'No, I think I am unharmed,' he said in a slow, precise voice, feeling his bones. 'But I have lost hold of my horse.'

The grey had indeed turned tail and departed whence it came. 'If you like we can go after him,' Lucy offered.

The boy clambered to his feet and dusted himself down carefully before saying, 'There's no need. He will only return to the stables.'

Now that he was standing up Lucy could see he was tall and painfully thin, with fair wispy hair and a pair of light blue eyes. 'You must be Ninian,' she remarked. 'I believe we are related, since I am married to your father's cousin, Philippe de Sevignac.' As soon as she spoke she remembered this was no longer true and flushed involuntarily, but the boy was not even looking at her. She went on hastily, 'May I offer you a lift? Perhaps to the drive . . .' She had no wish to be seen near the doors of Stansgate Park.

'Thank you, no. I was enjoying the walk. I would always rather walk than ride.' He made as if to continue on his way.

'But are you not concerned for your horse?'

'He may go to the devil, for all I care!' A faint colour tinged the pallid cheeks.

'I see,' said Lucy, thinking this fitted all too well with what she had been told of their heir to Stansgate Park. 'In that case I'll say goodbye, Ninian, and apologise again for upsetting your horse.'

He shrugged lightly, then stiffened. Following the direction of his gaze she saw Sir Ralph Stansgate approaching on horseback, leading the errant grey.

'So what have we here?' he asked softly, looking first at Lucy and then at Ninian, who was shifting uncomfortably from foot to foot. 'My fair cousin—and my unseated son! Or had you not noticed your horse was gone, Ninny?'

Ninian scowled. 'I was not unseated, Papa. I was leading my horse because he was lame and this—this lady startled him, so he ran off.'

'Miraculously cured of his affliction!' Sir Ralph's tone was scornful. 'He is certainly not lame now, so you may mount him again and ride beside me. Here—' He tossed the reins towards his son, who caught them but made no attempt to climb back on to his horse. 'What—can you not mount without a block? Lead him away, then, till you find a convenient tree stump.'

Sulkily Ninian led his horse along the path and Sir Ralph turned to Lucy. 'My son, as you see, takes after his mother's side of the family.' He smiled at her warmly. 'But this is an unexpected pleasure! What brings you to Stansgate? Has the necklace been found?'

Lucy shook her head. 'I came to visit your grand-mother.'

'Ah, the old harridan approves of you—well done! As long as her favour lasts you can do no wrong, but heaven help you if you should cross her in any way. Then you will learn just how intractable she can be.'

Lucy shivered slightly but said nothing.

'I must warn you that Letty was not at all pleased by your success at the Ball,' he went on. 'She has woken in the vilest of moods and is no doubt plotting your down-fall at this very moment. In short, she is out for your blood!'

'I did not expect to meet with her approval,' said Lucy, thinking that whatever revenge Lady Stansgate might devise it could be nothing compared with what had already befallen her.

'You have sinned on two counts,' Sir Ralph con-tinued, obviously relishing the situation. 'Not only did you trump her dismissal of you from the house by marrying into the family, but worse still you married Philippe, for whom she has always had something of a weakness.'

Lucy looked at him in surprise. He seemed quite untroubled by the admission. Perhaps he accepted it as tit-for-tat in view of his own affaire with Madeleine, if what Lady Emilie said was true.

'However, you need have no fear that it is returned.' He gave her a sly look. 'Though I believe at one time they may have been drawn together by mutual sym-pathy. On Philippe's part I doubt it was more than a momentary aberration. Where Letty is concerned it lingers on as a kind of romantic dream. She sees him as a poetic figure, ill-used by Fate, but if she were asked to share his bleak existence commonsense would soon prevail.' Allowing his horse to crop the grass he leaned across the pommel of his saddle. 'And what about *you*, Goddess? How long will *you* continue to flourish, I wonder, living a life of toil and hardship?'

She urged the mare forward. 'I am not afraid of hard work, Sir Ralph.'

Immediately he moved to seize hold of her reins, pulling the mare to a halt. 'But when winter comes? It won't suit you, Goddess, mark my words. You're a woman crying out to be cherished, dressed in the finest gowns and surrounded by a host of admirers. 'Tis a crime to lock you away—'

Angrily she snatched the reins from his grasp. 'You may have succeeded in appealing to Madeleine's vanity, Sir Ralph, but I am not so susceptible. I care nothing for fine clothes—'

'Or jewels?' he inquired with a cynical smile.

She hesitated, reminded suddenly of the discrepancy between his story and Philippe's. Yet Lady Emilie had implied that Sir Ralph knew more of Madeleine's life in France than Philippe . . .

'Don't be angry, Goddess. My only desire is to help you. If it is money you need you have only to ask.'

Had he won Madeleine by such mercenary lures? she wondered. Aloud she said, 'Thank you, Sir Ralph. I will inform Philippe of your kind offer.'

He gave a short laugh. 'He is too proud!'

'And so am I! Good day to you, Cousin.' Quickly she stirred the mare with her whip, thankful that this time he showed no sign of following her but was instead setting off in the opposite direction in pursuit of his recalcitrant son.

When they returned to Brooktye she found Mollie Thrupp alone in the kitchen, seated beside the stove. The woman looked up as she entered and said, with

open insolence, 'I've a message for you from *a friend*.'
She left a significant pause and then continued, 'He says
to remind you he's awaiting for you to tell him when the
coast is clear.'

Lucy controlled her anger with difficulty. 'Thank you,
Mrs Thrupp. I take it you are referring to Will Voller?
You may tell him I see no likelihood of the coast being
clear today. He will have to be patient a while longer.'

She left the room, aware the woman was staring after
her, and went into the drawing room so that she could be
alone to read Kitty's letter.

It was exceedingly difficult to follow, jumping from
one subject to another almost within the same sentence,
so typical of its author's butterfly mind. The gist, however, was that Kitty had by no means given up hope of
raising enough money to pay off her husband's debts and
secure his release from prison. So far she had managed
to obtain only half the sum required but she had not yet
exhausted the vast circle of family and friends upon
whom she felt entitled to call for help.

Lucy was filled with reluctant admiration for her
stepmother, who was so ready to sink her own pride in
appealing to people she had once considered her in-
feriors. She truly loves my father, she thought, and it was
wrong of me to blame her for his downfall. Kitty's letter
was full of remorse for her past indiscretions and made it
clear she was determined to atone by effecting Charles
Tennant's release.

'You do not mention the salary you receive, my dear
Lucy,' the letter concluded, 'and I realise it cannot be
great. Nonetheless if you can put by some little sum—*no
matter how small*—every bit will help. How I wish we
could resume our old life in London! James misses you
terribly and for my part I am become quite horridly *plain*
with boredom!'

Lucy smiled ruefully as she slipped the letter beneath

the blotter. As a housekeeper she might have received some pittance from which to save a little to give to her father, but as a wife she had none. As a wife . . . !

Her expression sobered as she remembered the reality of her situation.

When at last M. de Sevignac picked up the candle to light her upstairs that evening she had no need to pretend exhaustion.

'You look tired,' he remarked as they mounted the stairs. 'I hope you have not been working too hard?'

'No, but I have the most fearful megrim,' she said. It was not altogether a lie. She had been feeling increasingly sicker as the evening wore on.

When they reached her door he stopped and turned her round to face him, studying her closely. 'If only we could put back the clock . . .'

'Unhappily that is impossible.' She put out a hand to open the door. 'Please excuse me. My head is aching quite intolerably. I must bid you goodnight.'

He bowed stiffly. 'Goodnight, Madame.'

The hurt and bewilderment in his eyes were more than she could bear. She went quickly into her room and closed the door behind her.

Seconds later she heard his footsteps retreating.

CHAPTER
NINE

'I AM going out!'

Startled by his peremptory tone Lucy dropped her feather duster and stared at M. de Sevignac. 'Out?' she repeated.

'I trust you have no objection?' He was looking at her almost with dislike.

She turned away to avoid the accusation in his eyes. 'Of course not.'

'Aren't you even curious to know where I am going?'

She forebore to answer, moving towards the door, but he caught hold of her arm. 'I am sorry, I quite forgot to ask if you are quite recovered this morning?' His tone was provocative rather than concerned.

'I am perfectly well, thank you.' She pulled away from his grasp. 'Had you not better be on your way?'

She heard him swear under his breath and then the door slammed behind him. Leaning her head against the door jamb she gave way for an instant to her feelings, but almost at once came the realisation that this was the opportunity she needed. Where M. de Sevignac had gone she could not be sure, but guessed he might be paying a call on his cousin, perhaps to establish for certain that the Bride's Necklace had not been discovered at Stansgate Park after the Ball.

Pulling herself together, she turned back into the kitchen. 'Where is Junot?' she inquired of Mollie Thrupp.

The woman gave her a sullen look. 'Out in the

vineyard. The Frenchman's set him to mending holes left in the hedge by rabbits.'

'That should keep him occupied for a while.' She heard the rumble of wheels in the yard. 'M. de Sevignac has just left. Would you please go quickly and tell Will Voller that I wish to see him?'

A slow smile spread over Mollie's face. 'Is that so?' she said insolently. 'Oh, yes, ma'am . . . I'll go immediately. He'll be delighted, I'm sure!'

'There is no need to be impertinent, Mrs Thrupp. Just do as I say—and hurry!'

As soon as the woman had left the room Lucy paced up and down, planning her course of campaign. It was imperative that William should search every inch of the house, so that he might be satisfied the jewels did not exist. A momentary pang of doubt assailed her. Supposing Sir Ralph was right and Madeleine had not taken the jewels? But she dismissed it instantly. Wherever the jewels might be they were not in this house, she was certain, or M. de Sevignac would have made use of them long before now. Moreover, unless he were the finest actor in the world, he had already told her the truth.

She went up to her room, from where she could look down on the vineyard, and saw that Junot was working in a leisurely fashion. He would make the job last as long as he could, she felt sure. And if he returned while William was still in the house . . . ? Well, she would cross that bridge when she came to it.

The kitchen door slammed and Mollie's voice called gloatingly up the stairs, 'Someone to see you, ma'am. Says it was about time too—' She broke off as William shouldered her aside and came to stand at the foot of the stairs, looking up.

Lucy descended slowly. 'You may leave us, thank you, Mrs Thrupp.'

Muttering to herself, Mollie went.

'You've taken your time.' William accused. He looked somewhat better this morning, clean-shaven and wearing a cambric shirt Lucy thought she recognised as belonging to M. de Sevignac. A lock of stray hair fell across his forehead as she remembered, but the glittering blue eyes and twisted mouth belonged to a stranger, reminding her all too vividly that this was not the young and dashing William Forster but Will Voller, deserter and thief.

She said coldly, 'It wasn't safe for you to come before. M. de Sevignac has just gone out and the house is empty. You may search it if you wish, but only on condition you return the Bride's Necklace to me first. That was our agreement.'

'So it was.' He grinned. 'Unfortunately, I do not happen to have it about my person at this minute, so—' He sprang rapidly up the stairs, brushing her aside.

'William!' She hurried after him, almost tripping over the hem of her gown in her haste. 'I insist you give me back the necklace! If you do not fetch it at once I—I will call Junot. He is not far away. I shall tell him you broke into the house—'

'Go ahead,' he challenged, calling her bluff. 'Meanwhile I may as well start with the attic. Do you have a ladder?'

She hesitated, biting her lip. 'There's one there already,' she said reluctantly. 'We used it only the other day . . .'

'For what reason?' he demanded, immediately suspicious.

'We were looking for old clothes in a trunk. William, *please*—how do I know you will keep your side of the bargain?'

'How do *I* know you'll keep yours?' He tested the ladder for steadiness and started up it. 'We shall have to trust each other, shan't we?'

'Trust!' she echoed bitterly. 'How can I trust a man who deserted me for no good reason except that I turned out not to be an heiress?'

'I call that an excellent reason!' William retorted. He pushed open the trap door and peered into the attic. 'Now stop nagging and fetch me a candle. 'Tis confoundedly dark up here.'

Lucy sighed and did as he asked, though her mind was still busily trying to think of a way to make him give up the necklace. 'Take care,' she warned, as she handed up the candle and a tinder box. 'Some of the boards are rotten.'

She heard his muttered exclamation as he discovered the store of silks in Madeleine's trunk. He spent a while turning them over, then his footsteps sounded in other parts of the attic.

'You had best not take too long,' she called out. 'I do not know where M. de Sevignac has gone—'

'Go down and tell Mollie to give the alarm if someone comes,' he ordered.

Although she was loath to leave him unobserved she saw the sense in this. Indeed, she had no more wish than he to be caught red-handed, in the act of helping him search the house, so she ran swiftly down to the kitchen.

As she entered the room Mollie Thrupp thrust a bottle behind her skirts and guiltily wiped a hand across her mouth. Lucy said, 'I hope you are keeping your wits about you, Mrs Thrupp, for we have need of them. If my husband should return unexpectedly will you please come and warn us at once?'

Mollie glowered at her. 'Ain't one man enough for you, then? Why should I act as lookout while you sport yerself upstairs with my Will?'

Lucy flushed. 'I assure you I am doing nothing of the sort! This is purely a matter of—of business . . .'

'Ho, yes?' said Mollie sceptically. 'And what sort of

business might you be having with Will Voller, I ask
meself. Knowed you in the past, he said—which proves
what I been saying all along. You're no better'n I am, my
lady, for all yer fine manners.'

Lucy turned away, anxious to get back to William as
soon as possible, but Mollie pursued her, by now in full
spate.

'How d'yer think the Frenchman'd like it if I tole him
that his wife's been playing him false with Will Voller?'
Mollie's full lips quivered tremulously. 'It ain't fair! Oh,
I didn't expect nothing from the Frenchman, 'cos he's a
gent'man, an' I knew there could never be nothing in it.
But Will—that's different. He's *my* kind, not yourn . . .'

Lucy looked at Mollie's moist eyes and heaving
bosom, the purple bruise still visible on her neck, and
felt a stab of pity. 'Will Voller means nothing to me,
Mollie,' she said quietly. 'My only concern is to get him
out of this house as quickly as I can. While he's here he is
in danger, surely you can understand that? So please—
keep watch. It is for his sake I ask, not mine.'

Without waiting for an answer, she left the kitchen
and returned upstairs to find William coming out of her
own room. 'I could have told you there was nothing
hidden in there.' she said, a little tartly.

He raised an eyebrow. 'Do you imagine I would take
your word for it? Which room is the Frenchman's?'

She pointed to the door.

He searched the bare, cell-like room thoroughly,
opening the closet and feeling in the pockets of the few
garments hanging there. Then he turned his attention to
the marquetry box. 'Where is the key?'

'I have no idea.'

'Is there anything inside?' He picked it up and shook
it, not without some difficulty for it was heavy. 'I can't
hear a rattling.'

'Do you honestly believe,' she said scornfully, 'that

he'd keep anything of value in such an obvious place?'

He gazed at the box. 'There are such things as secret compartments . . .' From his pocket he took a small knife and inserted the blade beneath the lid. 'Fortunately there are ways of beating even the most ingenious locksmith at his own game, and by the look of it this is likely to present no—special—difficulty!' With his last words he prised open the lid.

Drawn by her own curiosity, Lucy moved forward to peer inside the box. Lined in crimson plush, it was empty—save for a piece of paper.

William took it out of the box. 'It is in French,' he said, scanning it quickly, and then translated, '"I am sorry, Philippe, but my need is greater than yours. M."'

She took the note from him and read it herself. '*Now* will you believe me? This is the very note that Madeleine left for her husband when she took the jewels!' As she spoke she was conscious of a great relief. So Philippe *was* telling the truth! Sir Ralph had been wrong . . .

'It's a trick!' William's face was flushed with anger. '*You* put it there, intending me to find it—'

'That's nonsense! If I had wanted you to find it I'd surely have produced the key.'

'They *must* be here!' He jammed down the lid. 'Come, Lucy—the truth. I am tired of your lies.'

She stared at him, her throat suddenly dry. 'Not until you give me the necklace,' she said hoarsely.

His eyes narrowed. 'So you *do* know where they are?'

'I am saying nothing more until you keep your side of the bargain.'

'How do I know this is not another of your tricks?'

'As you said, we shall have to trust each other.' Her confidence was beginning to return. She had him now, if only she could convince him she knew where the jewels were hidden.

He smiled. 'Can this be the prim little miss I married,

who wouldn't say boo to a goose? Oh, Lucy, you've
grown clever over the years. So now you would try to
play me at my own game?'

'If you have left the necklace at Mollie's cottage,' she
said coolly, 'had you not better make haste to fetch it
before my husband returns?'

'Your *husband* is already here,' he retorted, 'and fast
growing impatient!' With startling speed he reached out
a hand to grip her round the throat, his expression
changing in an instant to one of undisguised menace.

'William, please—' She tried to break free but his
grasp only tightened warningly.

'No more games. Show me where the stuff is hidden.'

Helplessly she tried to shake her head, but the pressure increased, cruelly constricting her breathing. Gazing
up at his face she saw it mottled with rage, the veins on
his neck standing out like whipcord, and realised she had
gone too far. This was the William that Mollie knew,
cruel and vindictive. What chance did she stand against
such a man? Even if Junot were within earshot she could
not utter more than a croaking cry. A cloud of faintness
swept over her. 'For pity's sake—'

William suddenly became alert, listening. 'What's
that?'

Dimly, through the roaring in her ears, she heard the
sound of hoofbeats approaching swiftly, clattering into
the yard, followed by raised voices as though Mollie
Thrupp, caught by surprise, was trying to warn them.

William's grip loosened and she staggered back
against the bed, holding her throat.

'Who is it?' he hissed.

Unable to speak, she could only shake her head.

He backed towards the door. 'If you blab I'll make
you sorry you're still alive. And don't think you've got
rid of me yet. I don't give up that easy.' He disappeared
swiftly.

Lucy made an effort to recover her senses. If he had meant to frighten her he had certainly succeeded. Thank God M. de Sevignac had returned in time!

Hastily she stooped to pick up Madeleine's note, which had fluttered to the floor during the struggle, and trust it back into the box, closing the lid. It refused to shut properly. He would know immediately it had been forced.

'Are you there, ma'am?' Mollie's voice came up the stairs, respectful, even a little servile. 'You have a visitor. 'Tis Sir Ralph Stansgate himself.'

Lucy tried to control her shaking hands. Never had she felt less ready to face Sir Ralph! Unsteadily she moved on to the landing, clutching hold of the balustrade for support. 'Just a moment,' she called out feebly. 'Tell him I'll be down directly.'

But he was already in the hall, staring up at her. 'Good God!' he exclaimed. 'What on earth—?' Mounting the stairs two-at-a-time he caught her as she swayed on the top step.

' 'Tis nothing,' she protested. 'A—a bad headache, that is all.'

He pulled aside the collar of her dress and stared critically at the marks on her neck. 'A strange headache that causes such bruising. Who has done this to you, Cousin?' He turned pale. 'Surely not Philippe—?'

'No! No, of course not.'

'He's an odd fellow, to be sure, but I never thought him capable—'

'I tell you, it was *not* Philippe!' she snapped. Then, seeing his face full of genuine concern, she added in a milder tone, 'I cannot explain. Please go . . . I wish to be left alone.'

'You must rest.' His eye fell on the open door to M. de Sevignac's chamber. 'In here will do. Sit on the bed while I fetch you some brandy.'

Helplessly Lucy obeyed him. He returned almost at once, followed by Junot and Mollie Thrupp, who peered in at her curiously. Sir Ralph took the glass from Junot and dismissed them with a wave of the hand. 'You may both go about your business. I will see to Madame.'

Lucy sipped the brandy. 'Thank you,' she said at last. 'I am quite recovered now, but I think I shall do as you say and rest for a while.'

'Oh, no! You don't fob me off so easily, my dear.' Sir Ralph sat down beside her and regarded her steadily. 'First of all, where is Philippe? 'Tis unlike him not to be here.'

She frowned, finding it difficult to think clearly. 'But I thought he went to see *you*—'

'To see me?' Sir Ralph shook his head. 'We should have met on the road.'

'Well, he did not actually say where he was going,' Lucy admitted. 'I only assumed he had gone to visit you.'

'Ah!' Sir Ralph sat back and watched while she continued to sip at the brandy. 'Take your time, my dear.'

Lucy tried desperately to assemble her confused thoughts. The temptation to unburden herself was considerable. Though she did not entirely trust Sir Ralph he was at least a sympathetic listener. Was that why Madeleine had turned to him? 'You are very kind,' she murmured gratefully.

He leaned towards her, saying in a confidential tone, 'I know your secret. Believe me, I only want to help you, Goddess.'

Startled, she looked up at him.

'That is partly why I came,' he went on. 'To warn you that Letty has ferreted out the truth about your father. She has discovered he is in a debtors' prison and is bursting to tell Philippe.'

Lucy felt a surge of relief. 'Is that all?' she breathed. 'But he knows already . . . he has always known—'

'All?' queried Sir Ralph sharply. 'So there is more?'

Lucy was silent.

'Someone has attacked you,' he went on quietly. 'I want to know who—and why.'

Her eye fell on the marquetry box. 'It—it was a thief,' she said. 'I came upon a thief . . . in this room. He was forcing open the lid of that box. I suppose he must have been looking for the jewels—so many people seem to think they are hidden in this house.' She was speaking quickly now, trying to make her story plausible. 'When I came upon him he was startled and turned on me. He—he tried to strangle me. If you had not arrived when you did I believe he would have killed me.'

'So he has only just left? Why did you not tell me this the minute I arrived? We might have caught him.' Sir Ralph rose to his feet and strolled over to the box.

Lucy remembered the note. 'There is nothing inside except a message from Madeleine,' she said hastily. 'It proves beyond doubt that she did take the jewels with her to France . . .'

Sir Ralph took out the slip of paper and read it. 'Well, well . . .!' he murmured.

'So you were wrong—'

He looked at her. 'You had time to read it, then, while you were struggling with the intruder?'

She flushed. 'He—he read it aloud.'

'Did he indeed? Why did you not call for help while he was doing so? Surely Junot—'

'I—I did call out, but Junot was too far away and Mrs Thrupp seemed not to hear.'

He replaced the note in the box and closed the lid as best he could. 'This proves nothing. Madeleine took the jewels—I already knew that. She hid them inside the chimney in the drawing room, wrapped in a cloth bag. When she and Armand left during the night they took the bag with them but did not open it until they were in the boat, on their way to the French coast. They found it full of stones. Philippe had tricked them.'

Lucy stared at him. 'How do you know all this?'

'Madeleine told me in a letter. She never forgave him for it—'

'*Forgave* him! Surely she was wrong to have taken them in the first place?'

'Perhaps. Though as his wife she was entitled to some support from him, and heaven knows he gave her little enough.'

'Why should he?' Lucy's tone was defiant. 'When she was expecting another man's child?'

Sir Ralph's gaze clashed with hers. 'Who told you that?'

'No matter.' Lucy's chin lifted, her strength beginning to return. 'But it explains why you may be somewhat biased in her favour. Perhaps she lied to you in her letters—'

'It was not in her nature to be devious. She was maddening in many ways, but never deceitful.' A muscle in his cheek twitched. 'Oh, yes, I loved her! She was very beautiful—and utterly wasted on Philippe. As you are, Goddess . . .'

'No, Sir Ralph!' Lucy stood up, still pale but rapidly regaining her composure. 'Pray do not try to divert me with any more idle compliments. I prefer plain speaking—'

'And so do I,' he agreed. 'So—speaking plainly, Cousin—I think you're being blackmailed.'

She stared at him.

'The signs are obvious,' he continued calmly. 'Come now, you can confide in me. Has it something to do with your father?'

'Of course not!'

'You need money, don't you? I wish you would let me help you.'

'It would take far more than any sum you may have imagined,' she said, thinking not of her father's debts but of William's desire to buy land.

'So you admit it?' He was triumphant. 'That's better! Now—how much?'

She bit her lip, furious with herself for falling into the trap.

Suddenly he turned his head towards the door, listening. Then he rose to his feet. 'If that is Philippe returning, as I suspect, we had better go downstairs. It might be a little compromising for us to be discovered here, in a bedchamber . . .'

So absorbed had she been in their conversation she had failed to hear the phaeton arriving in the yard. She turned white with apprehension.

Sir Ralph strode to the door. 'I will go down immediately. Follow me when you are ready. Are we to tell him the same story you told me, of an intruder?'

Wordlessly she nodded.

'Very well.' He gave her a rueful smile. 'I could wish he had not returned so soon. We must continue this conversation at some other time.'

She listened to his footsteps descending the stairs. Would Philippe believe her story? And what of William—dissatisfied still and capable of further violence. She shivered and drew the collar of her dress over the bruises on her neck.

CHAPTER
TEN

M. DE SEVIGNAC looked from one to the other, his face impassive.

'Heaven knows what would have happened had I not arrived when I did,' Sir Ralph said easily, sprawled on the sofa as if he were quite unaware of the tension in the atmosphere.

Lucy envied him his calm. Perched stiffly on the edge of her chair, she felt certain all her indecision and subterfuge must show in her face.

'The man is exceeding dangerous,' Sir Ralph went on. 'Look at the bruises on her neck . . .'

M. de Sevignac looked at the bruises on her neck. His expression did not alter. 'And you say you did not recognise him, Madame?' he inquired.

She shook her head, not daring to trust her voice.

He strode to the door, flung it open and called, 'Junot!'

''Tis these wretched jewels you will keep hidden on the premises,' Sir Ralph persisted with a sly smile. 'They are, I fear, a dreadful temptation to the local riff-raff. I wish you would give them to me for safe keeping.'

'There was only the Bride's Necklace, as you must know very well,' M. de Sevignac said calmly, 'and that has now—disappeared.' His gaze flickered to Lucy. 'It must have been something of a disappointment when the box was opened—'

'And only the note inside!' intercepted Sir Ralph. 'Yes, Cousin, I have to confess I have read it. Indeed, I am surprised you kept it, in the circumstances.'

'It serves to remind me how gullible I can be,' said M. de Sevignac, his eyes still on Lucy. 'A souvenir, nothing more.'

'What an odd fellow you are, to be sure.' Sir Ralph regarded him from under half-closed lids. 'You do not seem in the least concerned about what has happened to your poor wife. She was in a sorry state when I found her, I assure you.'

'On the contrary, I am very concerned—and I intend to get to the bottom of the affair.' He turned as Junot entered the room. 'I take it you are acquainted with what has happened?'

Junot's round face was creased with anxiety. 'Yes, Monsieur, and I must tell you how sorry I am that I did not come to Madame's aid, but the truth is I was working so hard in the vineyard that I—'

'You saw—and heard—nothing?'

'No, Monsieur.'

'And you've not noticed anyone suspicious near the house in the last few days?'

'No, Monsieur. It is true that idle good-for-nothing Will Voller startled Madame some days ago when he looked through the window, but I've not seen him since. And I have asked Mollie Thrupp, whose *bon ami* he is—' Junot tapped the side of his nose meaningly—'and she swears she has not seen him either.'

M. de Sevignac turned to Lucy. 'You did not recognise the man?'

'No.' It came out as a whisper.

'Then we must discount Will Voller. Thank you, Junot.'

'Monsieur, I would cut off my right arm rather than anything should happen to Madame! I am desolate . . . never again will I leave her alone in the house while you are away—'

'Thank you, Junot. And now you may see my cousin to the door.'

Sir Ralph raised an eyebrow. 'Am I dismissed?'

'I should like to speak to my wife alone. But I must of course thank you for . . . saving her life.' There was an underlying note of irony in the words.

Sir Ralph glanced at Lucy. 'If you take my advice you'll allow her to rest first. She's in no fit state to talk at present.'

'I shall show some consideration, I promise you.' He held out a hand to help his cousin to his feet. 'But I never asked you, Ralph, the purpose of your visit? My apologies for being so remiss.'

Sir Ralph brushed an imaginary speck of dust from his sleeve. 'Just a social call, Cousin. Well-timed, as it turned out.'

'Well-timed, indeed!'

Ignoring the jibe, Sir Ralph bent low over Lucy's hand. 'Goodbye, my dear. We shall meet again before too long, I hope.'

She looked into his yellow-flecked eyes and felt uneasy, certain he would not let the matter rest there. 'Goodbye, Sir Ralph. And thank you.'

As soon as he had left the room, escorted by Junot, she braced herself for the interrogation which must surely follow, but M. de Sevignac turned away from her to stare out of the window and said nothing for a full minute.

When at last he spoke it was with surprising gentleness and seemingly unconnected with the events that filled her mind. 'I went to call upon my grandmother today. She sends her warmest regards to you.'

It took her a moment to collect her thoughts. 'I see. I—I thought you had gone to visit your cousin.'

'Did you?' He appeared to consider this statement, then returned to his former subject. 'We talked of you a good deal—and of your life before you came to Sussex.'

She glanced at him quickly, but his expression was still calm, though watchful.

'I fear I've grown intolerably selfish over the past few years,' he went on. 'Junot had told me, of course, that your father was in a debtors' prison, but I hardly spared a thought for how you must feel. No doubt you are very concerned for him?'

She found it difficult to know how to reply. 'I am concerned, naturally, but my stepmother writes that he has now come to terms with his situation, insofar as this is possible. I do not know, however, whether his experience will persuade him to alter his way of life if he is ever released . . .' Her voice died away doubtfully.

'But you would like to help him if you could?'

'Of course, but I fear it is not possible.' She tried to follow his line of thought, but could only think how odd it was that both he and Sir Ralph should suddenly be filled with curiosity about her father. The connecting link struck her with sudden force. 'Of course—Cousin Letty! She has been to see your grandmother . . . but your grandmother already knew—'

'You are not being entirely honest with me, Madame,' he said gravely. 'This morning I found your stepmother's letter beneath the blotter on the escritoire and read the final page before I realised what it was. She appealed to you for help, did she not?'

'Yes, but—'

'How much do you need to pay off his debts?'

She shrugged helplessly. 'Kitty says she has managed to raise half the money needed, but there must be a thousand or more still to find.'

'Why did you not tell me of this?'

She flushed. 'What would have been the point? There is nothing you can do about it.'

He was watching her with a puzzled frown. 'You know

that personally I have no money to offer you?'

'Of course. It never entered my head—'

'But the Bride's Necklace . . . you might have considered that your property?' His tone was placatory,
almost pleading.

She stared at him uncomprehendingly. 'The Bride's
Necklace? What has that to do with it?'

'I am trying to understand, believe me!' With an effort
he controlled his impatience. 'Perhaps it was an accident. The clasp came undone while we were travelling
home and you put the necklace in your reticule for
safety. Only then did it occur to you that it might provide
a solution to your problems . . .'

She stared at him, horrified. 'You think I stole it . . .
to raise the money for my father?'

His expression was bleak. 'The temptation must have
been great—'

'No!'

'—And doubtless you hoped to divert my attention
from its loss by pretending a passionate response to my
advances—'

'How *dare* you!' Hot tears sprang into her eyes.
'You—you must know that was not pretence . . .'

'Must I? It seems to me that it fits all too neatly. The
trouble was, of course, that the necklace alone was not
enough, so you decided to look for the de Sevignac
jewels, even though I had already told you they did not
exist. No wonder you were so curious about them.' He
shook his head wonderingly. 'Yet you preferred to
believe the gossip you had heard in the town . . .'

She stood up, clenching her hands. 'You believe *I*
forced open the box! You think I was looking for the
jewels—that my stepmother's letter had prompted me to
take desperate action.' Feverishly she pulled down the
collar of her dress. 'Then how did I get these bruises? Do
you imagine I inflicted them upon myself, to make my

story more convincing?'

His eyes grew cold. 'I am giving you the chance to tell me the truth.'

The realisation that she was indeed *not* telling the truth swept over her. Her eyes clouded with guilt and she looked away from him. If only she could confide in him . . . But the danger was not yet over.

'My dear, I know my cousin too well,' he said evenly. 'Nothing you have to tell me will come as a surprise, I assure you.'

'But it has nothing to do with Ralph!'

With a suppressed oath he rose to his feet and resumed staring out of the window. 'When I walked into this house the atmosphere was thick with conspiracy. He offered you financial help, did he not?'

'Yes, but—'

'And when you would not take it then he tried to force you—'

'No!'

He swung round, his eyes dark with anger. 'Don't lie to me, Madame! I'm not blind, nor am I a complete fool. When I arrived Ralph was in this room, yet by his own admission he had been upstairs—had come upon you in my bedchamber and read the note left in the box. Why then should he be so anxious for me to find him downstairs unless he was trying to conceal something from me? And why should you have remained hidden until you had composed yourself sufficiently to face me— hiding the bruises on your neck?' His voice was harsh with contempt.

'I had had a shock—'

'Of that I've no doubt!' He passed his hand over his eyes, as if unable to bear the sight of her a moment longer. 'I don't entirely hold you to blame. I should have warned you more strongly, perhaps, what manner of man my cousin is.'

Lucy twisted her hands together nervously. 'I told you, it had nothing to do with Ralph.'

'Oh, come! Are you intending to revert to your tale of an intruder?'

Lucy flushed. 'Your cousin is quite innocent—'

'Innocent! That's hardly the word I should use to describe him.' His eyes narrowed. 'Do you take his part, then?'

'No, but you are quite wrong. If you'd only listen to me—'

'Why should I? Once I listened to Madeleine, her excuses, her self-pity, her lies . . . When she left for France, she was carrying Ralph's child, did you know that?'

'I—I had guessed that it was so.'

'And you would follow in her footsteps?' His face altered and he put out a hand to lift her chin, searching her eyes. 'I wanted to believe you were different . . .'

'I *am* different,' she protested.

'Then prove it by giving me back the necklace,' he said coldly, 'and we will forget the matter entirely.'

'I cannot—'

His gaze sharpened. 'You no longer have it? When you went into Cuckfield yesterday you met someone— by pre-arrangement . . .?'

She saw it was useless trying to convince him of her innocence. He had already seen the guilt in her eyes, even though it was not for the reason he supposed. All she could do now was retrieve the necklace from William, by whatever means possible, and restore it to its rightful owner. It would not put right all the wrongs between them, but it was the least she could do by way of atonement. 'No, I do not have the necklace,' she said quietly, 'but I will—'

He stopped her words with a savage kiss, holding her face between his hands so that she could not turn away.

When at last he drew back his eyes were full of loathing. 'Go away,' he muttered. 'I've grown heartily sick of Cousin Ralph's leavings. And for God's sake find a scarf to cover those bruises on your neck. They disgust me!'

She stood immobile, unable to speak.

'Go away!' he repeated, almost snarling the words.

She obeyed him, turning quickly and running from the room before the humiliation of tears overtook her.

Lucy sat in her room, staring unseeingly at the threadbare carpet. There was only one course of action open to her. It was quite simple. First, she must make William give back the necklace. Then she would leave Brooktye. After all, what was the point of her staying? The chances of ever becoming Philippe de Sevignac's wife in reality seemed more remote than ever. Besides, if she were gone perhaps William might be persuaded to abandon his search for the jewels and leave the district.

There came a knock at the door. Lucy swung round, suddenly filled with unreasonable hope, but it was only Mollie Thrupp who entered. 'Yes?' she said discouragingly. 'What is it?'

Mollie stared down at her with dark, resentful eyes. 'Will wants to see you again. Unfinished business, he says.'

Lucy sighed. 'You may tell him it's over. I am going away and so shall be of no further use to him.'

'Going away?' Mollie repeated, with obvious surprise. 'Why should you do that?'

'Oh, please don't pretend regret, Mrs Thrupp! I am sure you must be delighted at the news. As to why, you had best ask your friend Will Voller. It is he who has made it impossible for me to stay.'

Mollie was silent for a moment. Then she said. 'It won't suit him.'

'I daresay it won't, but he's left me with no alternative.'

'He can turn very nasty when he's crossed, can Will.' Her tone was fearful rather than threatening.

Lucy put a hand up to her neck and touched the tender skin. 'So I have already discovered.'

The woman's breath came in a sharp, indrawn hiss. 'You too?'

Lucy remembered the almost identical bruise she had seen on Mollie's neck. 'If he uses you so badly,' she said curiously, 'why do you help him?'

Mollie flushed a dull red. 'Got no choice, have I?'

'What do you mean? Does he have some hold over you?'

'He's my man. We'm bound together.'

'Bound together?' Lucy was puzzled.

Mollie tossed her head defiantly. 'That's the country way, Will says. He don't hold with no parson saying a few words over us in church. We'm bound together by blood.' She held out her wrists, pointing to a faint scar across the veins.

Lucy stared at her. 'So you think of yourself as his wife?'

Mollie bridled. 'I *am* his wife! That's why I got to help him, see?'

Lucy said slowly, 'Would you believe me if I told you that legally he has no hold over you at all?'

'Legal—what's legal?' Mollie scoffed. 'That don't mean anything.'

'On the contrary, it means a good deal.' She made a swift decision. After all, what did she have to lose? Mollie might even prove a useful ally once she realised she owed no loyalty to William. 'Has it not occurred to you, Mrs Thrupp, that he must have some hold over me as well? Otherwise why should I help him against my better judgment?'

Mollie's eyes narrowed. 'He says he was once your lover—that you're helping him so as he keeps quiet about it and don't tell the Frenchman.'

'That's partly true. But he wasn't only my lover—he was my husband. Indeed, in the eyes of the Law, he still is . . .'

Mollie Thrupp's mouth fell open slackly and her colour came and went.

'So you see,' Lucy persisted, 'you owe him nothing. He has not been entirely honest with you.'

Mollie pressed a hand to her side as if the news had winded her. 'It ain't possible!'

'I can show you my marriage lines to prove it, if you wish. He is a liar and a trickster, Mrs Thrupp—and we have both been his victims.'

'Ain't he clever, though,' Mollie said slowly. 'You got to admit he's clever. Tricking a lady like you into marriage—'

'I was only seventeen at the time,' Lucy protested, 'and knew nothing of the ways of men. William was in the militia . . .'

'An' he wound you round his little finger! Aye, he can talk a woman into anything, Will can.' A sly expression came into her eyes. 'So you was married all along! That won't please the Frenchman, I'll wager.'

Lucy began to feel uneasy. Mollie Thrupp was not reacting quite as she had expected. 'Never mind M. de Sevignac,' she said quickly. ''Tis Will Voller who concerns us at this moment. You say he's waiting to see me?'

'Aye,' said Mollie, her eyes darkening with suspicion.

'Then I must not disappoint him.' She rose to her feet. 'I will go to your cottage at once.'

'You said you was going away,' Mollie said accusingly.

'Not until after I've seen William. As he told you, we have unfinished business.' She went to the table beside her bed, intending to take out her father's travelling pistol. If she were to confront William again she would feel safer armed, though she had no intention of loading it, hoping that the mere sight of the weapon in her hands might persuade him to part with the necklace.

But when she opened the drawer it was empty. The pistol had disappeared, and with it the bag containing bullets and powder.

It was then she remembered seeing William come out of her room when he was searching for the jewels . . .

'What's the matter?' Mollie was watching her with a puzzled frown.

'Nothing.' Hastily Lucy shut the drawer. The thought that William might be in possession of the pistol filled her with misgiving. Yet surely he would not use it against a woman?

She shivered, remembering his hands around her throat; then turned resolutely towards the door. 'Please tell no-one where I have gone. It is important we are not interrupted.'

'I'm coming with you—'

'No!' She swung back to face Mollie, saying urgently, 'I must see him alone. Surely you can understand that?'

The woman regarded her with open hostility. 'You want him back. You're trying to steal my Will . . .'

Lucy realised that, though ill-used by William, Mollie still loved him and saw her only as a rival, not an ally. 'I promise you I do *not* want him back,' she said earnestly. 'It is M. de Sevignac I love, not Will Voller. My only concern is to persuade William to leave us alone.'

Mollie's sullen gaze wavered slightly.

Taking advantage of her hesitation, Lucy slipped from the room, praying that Mollie would not follow her—at least, not immediately. There might come a time when she would welcome an interruption, if William proved dangerous.

Junot was engaged in sweeping the yard and looked

up when she appeared, a concerned expression on his amiable face. 'Madame should not leave the house alone. It is not wise—'

'I shall be quite safe, Junot. There is no need to worry.'

As she turned away he called after her, 'Where you go, Madame? Why you not take the gig?'

She paused. 'Because I'm only going as far as Mrs Thrupp's cottage. There's no need—'

'Why you go there?' he demanded, frowning. 'Mollie Thrupp, she is in the house.'

'I know that, but there is someone else I wish to see.'

'I come with you!' Decisively he tore off his apron.

'No, Junot, I must go alone.' She hesitated. 'However, if I do not return within a half hour then you may come to look for me. Only—take care.'

Giving him no further chance to protest she walked on down the drive towards the dark, uninviting cottage hidden among the yews.

She knocked on the door. There was no answer so cautiously she pushed against it. It swung open with a creak. 'William?' she called.

Still no answer.

She stepped inside, wrinkling her nose in disgust at the smell of dirt mingled with stale cabbage, and found herself in a room filled with a jumble of shabby furniture. Dust lay thick everywhere and the remains of a frugal meal were on the table. She saw William immediately, slouched in a chair and apparently asleep.

The door swung to behind her with a bang. His eyes opened, focussing on her with difficulty. Instantly his expression grew wary and he struggled to his feet. 'What the hell—?'

'You told Mollie you wished to see me.'

'Aye, so I did.' He was swaying slightly and his breath

stank of rum. 'But I was not expecting you to come here . . .'

She perceived that for the moment she had the advantage and made haste to use it. 'I came to tell you I am leaving Brooktye, and so can be of no further use to you in your search. Moreover I mean to inform M. de Sevignac of your presence here and your intentions.' She saw his face darken and hurried on. 'I am giving you a chance to get away, William, before he learns the truth. Give me back the necklace—and then go!'

'Why should I?' He jerked his chin aggressively. 'I've done nothing wrong . . . yet.'

She swallowed. 'You broke into his house . . . and attacked his wife—'

'Only you're not his wife, are you?' he sneered. 'And I did not break into his house. You invited me in to look for the jewels. How would that sound in court?'

'You forced open the box—'

'But he thinks *you* did that. Mollie told me. That's a joke!' He gave her a long, calculating look. 'I believe you love him, your Frenchman. You would not wish to see him harmed?'

She turned pale.

'I thought not.' He gave her an unpleasant smile. 'But it would be all too easy, you know. You yourself have furnished me with the means.' He drew her father's pistol from his pocket.

Fascinated, she stared at the gleaming weapon in his hands. 'You wouldn't dare—'

'Wouldn't I? It may interest you to know I fully intend to make good use of it before too long. That is why 'tis already primed . . .'

She spoke through stiffened lips. 'What is it you want me to do?'

'You know well enough—' He broke off abruptly and she saw his expression change as his eyes travelled to the door behind her. 'Don't move,' he snapped, as instinctively she began to turn her head.

'What a touching scene!' The voice behind her was M. de Sevignac's. 'Such domestic harmony . . . so 'tis all true!'

CHAPTER
ELEVEN

HORRIFIED, Lucy realised that M. de Sevignac could not
see the pistol in William's hand because she was standing
between them, yet she dared not move an inch or take
her eyes from William's face.

Sweat had broken out on his brow but the hand
holding the pistol was steady enough. 'If you come any
further I shan't hesitate to shoot her,' he muttered
between clenched teeth.

Behind her M. de Sevignac said calmly, 'And what is
that to me? She is your wife, not mine.' In the same
instant he dealt her a swift blow in the back, sending her
sprawling halfway across the room and on to her knees.

A shot rang out. She turned swiftly to see a thin trickle
of blood dribbling from a graze above M. de Sevignac's
right temple. Thank God her father's pistol fired to the
right! She had often heard him complain of it, but could
only now be thankful he had never had it corrected.

By the look on William's face he had tumbled the
error, but before he had time to recover M. de Sevignac
launched himself forward, knocking William off balance. The weapon fell to the floor and spun into a
corner, out of reach.

Lucy watched, transfixed, as the two men rolled on to
the floor, each trying to gain mastery over the other. Of
the two M. de Sevignac was the heavier in build, though
there was not an ounce of superfluous flesh on his lean
frame and his outdoor life had given him muscles of

steel. William, on the other hand, had the extra strength that comes from a sense of fanatical purpose. His face contorted with rage, he sought to gain a hold on M. de Sevignac's throat, and each time this satisfaction was denied him he gave a snarl of rage before throwing himself once more into the offensive.

M. de Sevignac was rapidly becoming impeded by the blood running down over his eye and every now and then was forced to wipe it away with his sleeve. Quick to take advantage of this weakness, William at last succeeded in delivering a blow that knocked his opponent to the floor and threw himself upon him, this time achieving a stranglehold that looked to be fatal.

Lucy searched wildly for a weapon, but just as her fingers reached for the discarded pistol she saw Junot appear in the doorway, his face white with fear and an ancient blunderbuss of French design held in his trembling hands. 'Stop—or I fire!' His voice, though shaky, was determined.

Startled, William looked over his shoulder and saw the weapon. Instantly he released his grip on M. de Sevignac's throat and reeled back against a table, which gave beneath his weight so that he was thrown to the ground.

M. de Sevignac got to his feet, albeit a little unsteadily, and seized William from behind, wrenching his arms behind his back. 'Bravo, Junot!' he said, breathless from his exertions. 'That was very well done.' His eyes took in Lucy's pale face as she stood by the door. 'Indeed, we seem to have caught ourselves a pretty pair of conspirators.'

Lowering the blunderbuss, Junot gazed at Lucy with unhappy eyes.

'You'd best tell Mrs Thrupp 'tis safe to come in now.'

She entered at once, needing no bidding, and went straight to William. 'Oh, Will, it weren't none of my doing. 'Twere hers—' She darted a venomous look at Lucy. 'Your *wife's*!'

William made a half-hearted attempt to free himself, but M. de Sevignac jerked back his arms so violently that he cried out in pain.

'Will Voller, William Forster . . . Whatever you choose to call yourself,' he hissed into his captive's ear. 'Between us we've enough evidence to put you away for years, if not to hang you. Now, where is the necklace?'

William remained silent, no longer struggling, his eyes lowered.

'There is no point in lying,' M. de Sevignac said coldly. 'It is quite clear to me now that your wife stole the necklace and brought it to you here. So—tell me where it is hidden.'

Still William said nothing.

'Pick up the pistol, Junot, and keep him covered.'

With his gaze fixed fearfully on William, Junot did as he was told. M. de Sevignac relaxed his hold and William stood sullenly rubbing his arm.

M. de Sevignac appealed to Mollie. 'Come now,' he said persuasively. ''Tis *your* home—you must know where the necklace is hidden.'

Molly cast an uneasy glance at William. 'He said nothing to me about the necklace,' she admitted grudgingly.

'Even so, you must have some idea where he would choose as a hiding-place,' M. de Sevignac persisted.

Mollie looked uncertain. 'If I find it for you, will you let Will go free?'

M. de Sevignac shrugged. 'Why not?' His gaze flickered to Lucy, who was standing as if turned to stone, her eyes fixed on his face. ''Tis all he has filched from me that I value.'

Again Mollie looked at William. He gave her a barely perceptible nod and she disappeared from the room.

'Junot, give me the weapon.' M. de Sevignac held out his hand.

Junot obeyed him, side-stepping round the room to avoid coming close to William.

M. de Sevignac glanced down at the pistol. 'I thought I had seen it somewhere before. This at least should have made me suspicious, if nothing else.'

At last Lucy found her voice. 'You are quite wrong, Monsieur! I am not his accomplice. Truly I thought he was dead—'

'Quiet! I have had enough of your lies.'

William shot her a malicious look.

'Madame is telling the truth!' Junot's round eyes blazed with indignation. 'She thinks he is dead . . . I know it is so! When he look through the window she does not recognise him. I am there—I see how she is frightened.'

'You always were a fool where women are concerned, Junot.' M. de Sevignac added, with bitter self-mockery, 'And so am I, it seems.'

'But you cannot send her away!' Junot protested.

'I think she will leave soon enough of her own accord when she realises I can no longer be duped by her play-acting.' His gaze slid contemptuously over her, resting for an instant on the swell of her bosom above the slender waist; then moved away as Mollie re-entered the room. 'Ah, 'tis found . . .!'

With some reluctance Mollie handed him the Bride's Necklace. He held it up to catch what little light could penetrate the dirty window-panes and as its sparkling brilliance illuminated the gloom William took a step forward. M. de Sevignac at once raised the pistol warningly, at the same time slipping the necklace out of sight beneath his shirt. 'If you want your freedom,' he said coldly, 'you had best go now, before I change my mind.'

William stared at him with angry, frustrated eyes.

Then he went, pushing Mollie Thrupp roughly aside as he passed her in the doorway. She turned at once to follow him, calling, 'Will! Will, I only did it to save you. Don't turn against me, Will . . .'

As her voice faded away, Lucy appealed once more to M. de Sevignac. 'Philippe—'

'You too, Madame!' he snapped.

'No.' She spoke quietly but firmly. 'If you choose not to believe me, that is your affair, but the man who calls himself Will Voller is nothing to do with me. I cannot recognise in him the man I married when I was seventeen and he has no further hold over me, now that you know the truth. I'll go, if that is what you wish, but only when I am packed and ready—not hastily, like a thief in the night.'

He stood for a moment, gnawing his lip, then swung on his heel and left the room.

'Oh, Madame . . .' Junot's voice was full of sympathy. 'You must give him time. He will believe you again, you will see.'

'I wish I could share your optimism, Junot,' said Lucy sadly.

'Come, let us leave this horrible place. It has not a nice smell!' He held out his arm. 'I will take you home . . .'

They walked in silence up the rutted drive to Brooktye. When they reached the courtyard Lucy gave a heavy sigh. 'I am sorry, Junot. I fear I've been a disappointment to you. Your intention was a good one, but I was not the right choice, after all.'

'*Mais non!*' He stamped his foot in a sudden display of Gallic temperament. 'It is not so! You *are* the right person for Monsieur. You make him happy. One day we will all be happy together when we are in France. You will see!'

She shook her head regretfully. 'I fear not. One day you and he may return to France, but there will be no place in your future for me.' She glanced at the house but there was no sign of M. de Sevignac. 'I will go straight to my room and pack. I hope he will not object if I stay until tomorrow morning. It is far too late in the day to catch the stage back to London.'

'Madame, I wish to help you!' Junot's face was pale with resolution. 'If it is money you want—'

'No, Junot.' Gratefully she put a hand on his arm. 'Thank you for your concern, but there is nothing you can do.'

Unhappily he watched her go, his eyes thoughtful.

Once in her room she pulled her valise from under the bed and opened a drawer to take out her few possessions, but no sooner had she packed one nightgown and a chemise than she was overcome with the realisation she must leave Brooktye and sank on to the bed in a mood of black despair. She loved the house, for all its shabbiness and lack of comfort, and the countryside had become familiar to her. Most of all, she loved its master, and the thought that she must leave him with only harsh memories of her was almost unbearable.

For a long while she sat staring vacantly in front of her, until at last she was roused by the sound of carriage wheels in the drive below. Not Sir Ralph again, she prayed, for the situation was bad enough without his returning to make it worse.

But the voice she heard as she opened the door was high, imperious and undeniably female. Lady Stansgate! What business could she possibly have with them now? Cautiously she crept on to the landing, straining to hear the conversation below.

Junot's voice floated up the stairs, sounding anxious. 'But, my lady, I regret it is impossible. My master shuts himself away because he have much work to do and cannot be disturbed—'

'But surely when you tell him who it is—?'

'I already knock on the door. He make no answer.'

There was a pause. 'Very well, then. I will speak to your mistress, since my business is chiefly with her.'

'My mistress also cannot be seen. She has gone to her room.'

'Well, here's a pretty kettle of fish, to be sure! Each in his own room and cannot be disturbed . . . What has happened, I should like to know?'

'It's all right, Junot—I'll come down.' Hastily Lucy smoothed her hair and tried to pinch some colour into her cheeks. She descended the stairs slowly. 'Please show Lady Stansgate into the drawing room.'

Facing her visitor in the gathering dusk Lucy was reminded of their first encounter and thought how strange it was that the episode should end as it had begun, with Lady Stansgate's open hostility. 'You told Junot you wished to see me?'

'Certainly I do.' The blue eyes were cold as ice-chips. 'It is about time you realised that at least one member of this family has not been taken in by your cunning tricks, Madame. Your mask of gentility does not deceive *me*, I assure you—'

'Lady Stansgate,' Lucy interrupted, 'I have not the slightest notion what you mean, but in any case you have no need to worry. I am leaving Brooktye in the morning.'

Lady Stansgate registered astonishment, followed by consternation. She rapped out sharply, 'Where are you going?'

Lucy shrugged. 'To London, I suppose. There is nowhere else—'

'London!' An angry flush stained Lady Stansgate's marble countenance. 'So *that* is your plan . . . You mean to join him there, no doubt.'

Bewildered, Lucy stared at her.

'I see it all! Ralph is such a fool where women are concerned. Presumably he has offered you money to pay your father's debts?'

'Her father's debts are paid, but not by Ralph.'

They both turned to look at the speaker. M. de Sevignac was propped against the doorway as if too weary to stand upright, his face set in deep lines and the graze on his temple still evident. 'You are far too late, Letty, and quite misinformed as to the true facts. It is Grandmère, acting on my behalf, who has provided the money to secure Charles Tennant's release from gaol.'

The colour drained from Lucy's face. 'You did not tell me this! But why—?'

He glanced at her and said wryly, 'Because I, fool that I was, believed your actions were prompted by concern for your father. Now, of course, I know differently.'

'*You* may have come to your senses, Philippe,' said Lady Stansgate, two bright spots of colour appearing on her cheeks, 'but I fear that Ralph is still bewitched. I take it you are aware he has been conducting a clandestine affaire with your wife?'

M. de Sevignac detached himself from the doorpost and moved to lean instead against the mantelshelf. 'I doubt if it has gone that far, Letty,' he said with a sigh. 'I admit that yesterday I was inclined to be of the same opinion, but—'

'And how else must I learn of it but from my own son?' Lady Stansgate interrupted angrily. 'Poor innocent lamb, forced to witness an assignation only a few yards from his home! The child was shocked to his very depths!' She raised a snowy kerchief to dab at her eyes. 'And when I told Ralph of the sordid background whence she comes he is not in the least dismayed, but only informs me that he means to help her disreputable father!'

'I have already explained that will not be necessary.'

'Indeed,' Lady Stansgate continued inexorably, 'it would not surprise me if she were in some way responsible for the mysterious disappearance of the Bride's Necklace.'

'The necklace has been found,' M. de Sevignac said shortly. 'It was merely mislaid.' He frowned. 'Letty, we have had a very trying day. I should much appreciate it if—'

'My poor Philippe.' Lady Stansgate laid a gloved hand sympathetically on his arm. 'Once again we find ourselves companions in misfortune, betrayed by our own good natures. Shall we ever learn our lesson, I wonder?' Her eyes were fixed on him hungrily, her sharp features for once miraculously softened.

'I am sorry, my dear, but I must ask you to leave.' He patted her hand awkwardly and then removed it from his arm. 'I cannot discuss the matter further.'

'I understand.' She cast a meaning look at Lucy. 'I will come again in a little while, when you have had time to recover from the shock.'

Too weary to protest, he took her to the door.

When it was opened Junot all but fell into the room, regarding Lady Stansgate with a baleful glare.

'Please escort her ladyship to her carriage,' M. de Sevignac requested.

'It will be a pleasure, Monsieur!'

As she swept past him Lady Stansgate bestowed on Junot a look that said plainly had he been *her* servant she would have dismissed him instantly for insolence.

When the door closed behind them the room seemed ominously silent. M. de Sevignac stood staring at the floor, plunged in thought.

Lucy took a deep breath. 'It is kind of you and your grandmother to try and help my father, but perhaps in the circumstances—'

'It is already done.'

'So soon? But surely the payment can be stopped?'

'What is the point? At least it will mean you have somewhere to go.' His voice was flat, unemotional.

She reflected briefly that the last thing she wanted was to live with her father and stepmother again, but only said, 'I cannot possibly allow your grandmother to provide the money. When she knows how I deceived you . . .'

He raised his eyes to look her full in the face for the first time. 'She will probably not believe it. Grandmère prides herself as a judge of character and you already stand high in her estimation. I doubt very much if anything she is told will shake her faith in you.'

Lucy felt perilously close to tears. 'I—I hope that you will at least believe I am not in any way guilty of encouraging your cousin? We met by chance in the grounds of Stansgate Park when I was on the way back from visiting your grandmother and Ninian lost hold of his horse. Nor was it Ralph who administered these bruises on my neck but William, as you must now realise.'

He nodded, his expression sombre.

'The only reason I helped William search for the jewels was that I hoped he would then leave us alone.' The words came quickly now, tumbling over each other in her haste to explain. 'He wanted a great deal of money so that he might go north and buy land. The Bride's Necklace was not enough, but when he found it on the ground the night it was lost he kept it, to buy my silence. It was then I—' She faltered, seeing the disbelief written clearly on his face, and concluded lamely, 'It was then I discovered he was still alive . . . that I was not your wife after all.'

He remained silent, looking at her.

She gripped the back of the sofa. 'How could I know what manner of man he was? Oh, I can see it well enough now, but as a young girl I was wholly taken in by his lies and his declaration of love. Even the uniform helped to deceive me. Surely you can understand?'

'Oh yes, I understand. I too have been taken in by lies and declarations of love—'

'By Madeleine—not by me!'

'I was not thinking of Madeleine. She never pretended to love me. In that respect, at least, she was honest.'

'And so am I! Oh, what can I say to convince you?' Despairingly she pressed her hands against her wet eyelids.

'I fear there is nothing you can say—or do—that will make me change my mind.' He turned towards the door. ''Tis pointless to prolong this interview. Junot tells me you mean to take the stage for London in the morning?'

'If that is what you wish . . .'

'Wishes are a thing of the past where I am concerned. From now on I mean to occupy myself only with reality.'

She was silent.

'I will bid you goodbye, Madame, since I may not see you in the morning. I hope you have a comfortable journey.'

Such stilted pleasantries were more than she could bear. Choking, she turned away, but he had already closed the door behind him and did not witness her total surrender to grief.

Lucy and Junot dined alone, in melancholy silence, and she excused herself early to retire to her room. Once there, however, she made no effort to prepare for bed, but sat beside her half-packed valise, lacking the will or the energy to do anything but contemplate the bleak future awaiting her in London.

Was there no hope at all? Must she be banished for ever from the sight of the man she loved?

'There is nothing you can say—or do—that will make me change my mind . . .'

Suddenly she rose to her feet and began to undress, folding her gingham gown with care and placing it in her valise. When she was naked she drew on her nightgown, the tear at its neck now neatly mended, but this time took care to leave the ties unfastened. Then she sat at her dressing-table and unloosed her hair. It fell about her shoulders like a vivid, fiery mantle. With slow, measured strokes she brushed it until it shone. This done, she removed the valise into a corner of the room and sat down upon the bed to wait.

It was almost an hour before she heard M. de Sevignac's footsteps on the stair. Quickly she moved to the door and opened it a few inches. 'Monsieur,' she whispered urgently. 'Please—I must speak to you . . .'

After a brief hesitation he came along the landing towards her, holding the lamp aloft. 'Yes?' he said, in a far from encouraging tone. 'What is it?'

'It—it is rather private.' She opened the door a little wider, at the same time stepping back into the shadows of her room.

He approached cautiously. 'I warn you, Madame—if this is one of your tricks . . .'

'No, I—there is something I must say to you before I go.' Lucy swallowed nervously. Now that he was here her courage was beginning to fail. She was acutely aware of his height and maleness dominating the small room. 'Can—can you not close the door?'

His eyes narrowed. Nonetheless he did as she asked. 'Well?' he demanded. 'What lies do you have ready this time?'

'No lies,' she assured him earnestly. 'Only the truth. Philippe, please don't send me away! Let me stay as your housekeeper . . . as your mistress, if you wish.' She moved closer to him, putting both hands pleadingly

against his chest and lifted her face to his. 'I don't care
what people say . . .'

A nerve twitched in his jaw but his expression remained unmoved. 'Very prettily done,' he said, lightly
taking her wrists and holding her away from him.
'Though perhaps a trifle over-played.'

Desperately she sought for a chink in his armour.
'Why do we not return to France? You are in exile here
and cling to the vineyard as your only link with the past.
They say that Napoleon looks favourably upon members
of the *ancien regime* who wish to restore their lands to
prosperity. We could make a fresh start there and
no-one would know that we are not truly man and wife.'

He smiled grimly. 'An attractive idea, but I fear
impractical. Without money such an enterprise would be
impossible.'

'Surely if your grandmother is prepared to help my
father she would be only too glad to help her own
grandson?'

'Your father's debts, substantial as they may seem to
you, are a mere drop in the ocean compared with what I
should need to return to France.'

'But if you still have the jewels,' she persisted, 'surely
their sacrifice would be justified for this cause, if for
nothing else?'

His eyes grew cold as steel. 'Ah, there we have it! A
clever ruse, Madame, but you are still wrong. The de
Sevignac inheritance has already returned to France and
no trick of yours will alter that fact.'

'But your cousin told me that Madeleine wrote to him
after she returned to France. The bag in which she had
hidden the jewels contained only stones. She thought
you had tricked her—'

'And you would rather believe Ralph than me?'

'Of course not! But you could be mistaken. After all,
why should she lie? You said yourself she was honest.'

He regarded her with scorn. 'Do you seriously believe that if I had the jewels I would be working myself to death to raise a few paltry vines in an intemperate climate? Use your head, Madame!'

She could only gaze at him helplessly, her last ounce of hope draining away.

His eyes slid down to where her nightgown, only loosely fastened, had slipped from her shoulder, unnoticed in her agitation. His lips tightened. 'If you are seeking to distract me by this tempting disarray you are playing a dangerous game.'

Lucy said nothing, but kept her eyes fixed on his, making no attempt to cover herself.

'On the last occasion I visited your bedchamber,' he remarked conversationally, 'you put on a most convincing display of modesty. Yet now, if I am not mistaken, you would offer yourself to me without a single qualm?'

She moistened her lips. 'If you want me, Philippe,' she said in a low voice, 'I am yours . . .'

'No, Madame! It does not suit you to play the harlot.'

Stung by the contempt in his voice, Lucy retaliated, 'Am I so much more repulsive to you than Mollie Thrupp?'

His eyes snapped with anger. 'I have never taken Mollie Thrupp to my bed, whatever impression she may have contrived to give you. Good God, do you imagine I am quite lacking in discernment—to say nothing of a sense of smell?'

Her rage evaporated, to be replaced by desperation. If she antagonised him now, all was lost. 'Philippe,' she begged, close to tears, 'Stay with me, please . . .'

'Why do you ask that *now*, when it is too late?'

'Because I love you,' she said simply. 'I cannot bear to leave without showing you how much . . .'

He stared at her for a long moment in silence. When he spoke again his tone was grave. 'I will admit there was a time when I found myself in some danger of falling in love with you, but I suppose that was hardly surprising. You are a beautiful woman and I had been alone too long. My need for you became almost a fever, making it impossible for me to think of anything else.' As if unconscious of his actions, he put out a hand to touch her cheek, lightly stroking two fingers against the softness of her skin. 'Perhaps I could forget you more easily—'

Lucy caught hold of his hand and pressed it to her lips. 'But I do not want you to forget me!'

'I must!'

The anguish in his voice gave her courage. She held his hand against her wildly beating heart, staring up at him. 'What can I do to prove I am telling you the truth?'

For answer his mouth came down on hers, fiercely demanding. Yet his hands were gentle as they slipped the nightgown from her body, carried her to the bed and began caressing her with such exquisite tenderness she cried out with wonder. There was no further need for words as they came together at last in a surge of ecstasy all the more potent for its underlying sense of bitter-sweetness, of paradise gained and lost in the same moment; and finally fell asleep in each other's arms, sated and spent.

When Lucy stirred again she felt his arm still lying heavily across her breasts and smiled to herself. Now he cannot possibly send me away, she thought. She turned to study his face where it lay on the pillow beside her, illumined by the rosy glow of the rising sun. He looked strangely young in sleep, the deep lines on either side of his mouth relaxed, dark lashes fanned out against his cheeks like a child's.

As if sensing her scrutiny he opened his eyes and for a long minute they stared at each other in total awareness, acknowledging without speech all that had passed between them. Then he saw the warm light flooding the room and frowned. 'Surely it cannot be dawn already . . . ?'

Lucy smiled. 'All too soon, my love. But you need not go—'

Ignoring her outstretched hands, he leapt from the bed and strode over to the window.

Lucy shivered. 'Philippe, what is it—?'

When he turned to face her she was silenced by the expression on his face, which changed swiftly from stunned disbelief to a mask of mingled horror and loathing. 'So *that* is why you sought to distract me!' he began; then hurriedly snatched his clothes from the floor and began to pull them on.

Bewildered, Lucy sat up, clutching the bedclothes to her. 'I don't understand . . . what is the matter?' Gradually she became aware that the light coming in through the window was not after all the breaking dawn but a flickering reddish glow that filled the room. Her eyes widened. Clutching the sheet to cover her nakedness, she slipped from the bed and ran to the window. Incredulously she stared down at the blazing vineyard, then flung open the window and leaned out to get a better sight of the flames leaping high into the darkness. Immediately she began to choke on the drifting smoke and unmistakable smell of burning wood and vegetation. Hastily she closed the window again and swung round to face M. de Sevignac. 'Philippe, you must believe—'

But he had already gone from the room.

With trembling hands she dressed in the gown she had so carefully packed the night before, and flew down the stairs after him.

When morning came the scene was one of grim destruction. The barn was burned down and part of the stables, though they had managed to stop the fire from spreading to the house. The vineyard, however, was ruined. Torn from their supports, the wines lay charred and bleeding on the ground, trampled into a messy pulp that covered the entire field.

William had taken his revenge.

CHAPTER
TWELVE

Lucy sat beneath a cedar tree on the flowing lawns of the
Dower House and pretended to read a novel. From time
to time she sighed restlessly and gazed along the drive
leading to the main gates of Stansgate Park, before
dropping her eyes to begin again the passage she had
read five times already.

Beside her sat Lady Emilie, dozing a little in the
drowsy peace of a summer's afternoon. The air was still
and quiet, the silence broken only by the droning of a
bee plundering the honeysuckle and the sharp song of a
blackbird perched on a nearby ash tree. Everything
seemed to be waiting.

Over a week had passed since that terrible night when
they had fought to save Brooktye from total destruction,
and during that time no-one had set eyes on M. de
Sevignac. Not even Junot, who rode over daily from
Brooktye to report that his master was still locked in his
room, seemingly bent on disposing of the legacy of the
vines until the last drop was consumed and memory
destroyed. 'I must go to him,' was Lucy's immediate
reaction: but each time Lady Emilie had laid a restrain-
ing hand on her arm and cautioned her to be patient.

'I know my grandson,' she said. 'He is best left alone
until this crisis is passed.'

'But he does not know I am here,' Lucy reminded her
unhappily. 'He may even believe I have returned to
London—'

'My dear, in his present state I doubt he is capable of

such logical thinking. You would only remind him how much he has lost and aggravate his sense of futility. 'Tis better to wait.'

'I cannot impose upon your hospitality for ever. I have no right—'

'On the contrary, you have every right,' retorted the old lady. 'You are the only woman for my grandson, as I recognised immediately.'

Lucy shook her head. 'But I am not his wife—can never be . . .'

'Nonsense! 'Tis merely a matter of extricating you from this disastrous alliance.'

'How can that be done, now that William has disappeared?'

'He will be found.' Lady Emilie patted her arm. 'I am only thankful you had the good sense to come to me.'

Looking at her now, Lucy was filled with grateful affection. She had not known where to turn on that dreadful morning after the fire. They had fought all night side-by-side, desperately trying to save the house, and then M. de Sevignac had simply walked away from her, ignoring her pleas, and locked himself in his room. When he did not reappear she became convinced it was her own presence that disgusted him and knew she must leave, yet she could not bring herself to go too far away.

And so she had turned to Lady Emilie, telling her the whole story and seeking her help. Lady Emilie had listened gravely and for a while been silent; but at last she had merely chided Lucy for her foolishness and ordered her to stay until the coil could be straightened out. That it *would* be straightened out she seemed convinced. Unhappily it was a conviction Lucy could not share.

Nonetheless she had to be content for the time being to take each day as it came, hoping that by some miracle he would have a change of heart and agree to see her. Then perhaps she could convince him of her love, persuade him even now to let her stay and help him rebuild his life.

Her eyes drifted once more to the drive. Still it was empty. She found it intolerable, not knowing what was happening at Brooktye. If only Junot would come for her . . .

'It is odd Ralph has not been to see us.'

Lucy jumped at the sound of Lady Emilie's voice. 'I—I thought you were asleep, Grandmère.' She flushed. 'I am sorry. I keep forgetting I have no right to call you that.'

'Don't be silly, child. 'Tis only a matter of time.'

Lucy shook her head. 'I fear it will take a good deal more than time.'

'Then we must leave it to Ralph. After all, it is *his* land that has been damaged. He will see to it that the offender is brought to justice.'

'But he has not yet returned from London. Very possibly he does not even know what has occurred.'

'Of course he knows!' The old lady snapped open the fan which lay in her lap and began to use it vigorously. 'I realise you have a low opinion of him, my dear, perhaps with good cause. All the same, I think you will find him not unmindful of his duties where the estate is concerned.'

'My opinion of him is by no means low,' Lucy protested. 'I believe that in his own way he has tried to be kind—'

'—Even if his motives are somewhat questionable,' Lady Emilie concluded with a smile. 'Ralph is a strange mixture. So are both my grandsons, for that matter. It is no use expecting either of them to act in an entirely predictable manner.'

'No, indeed,' Lucy agreed with a sigh. 'Have you had

an opportunity to read the letter I received this morning from my stepmama?'

The old lady pursed her lips, 'I have read it, yes.'

'I know her style is somewhat effusive,' said Lucy, 'but I think her sentiments are genuine enough. She is very grateful to you . . . and so am I.'

'Well, we must hope she realises her own extravagance has been partly to blame for your father's downfall,' said Lady Emilie sententiously. 'Though by the tone of her letter I doubt it.'

'I am afraid she does encourage him,' Lucy admitted, 'but he was always a gambler. My mother was a strong influence for good while she was alive, but after her death it was almost inevitable he should give way to temptation. It is like a drug to him, I think. He simply cannot resist the excitement of the tables.'

Lady Emilie sniffed. 'Perhaps a longer spell in prison would have done him good after all. Nonetheless Philippe was of the opinion that we should do something about it, for your sake, and together we devised a scheme whereby he could raise the money against certain securities.'

'Securities?' Lucy repeated, puzzled.

'Some provided by me and the rest—' The old lady sighed. 'Of course, at that time he was convinced it was you who had taken the Bride's Necklace. He thought if he could tell you that your father's debts would be repaid then you would return the necklace.'

Lucy stared unseeingly at the honeysuckle. 'If he truly believed I had stolen the necklace and yet was prepared to forgive me—why, it is almost as though he loved me after all . . .'

'I am certain of it,' Lady Emilie declared. With a sidelong glance at Lucy she added, 'He also assured me the necklace was all he had. Moreover he looked me straight in the eye when he said it, and I believe he could not have done that unless his conscience was completely clear.'

Lucy turned to look at her. 'Then it was Sir Ralph who lied? Or Madeleine . . . ?'

'Not necessarily.' Lady Emilie leaned back in her chair, wearing an enigmatic smile. 'I have given a deal of thought to this puzzle over the last few days and it seems to me there are certain factors we have not taken into consideration. We have leapt to the obvious conclusions and been proved wrong.'

'But if it was not Philippe who exchanged the jewels for stones . . . ?'

'*Think!* Who else was there on that night?' urged the old lady.

'Madeleine's brother, Armand. But he would not have taken them from his sister . . . he would have used them to help her.'

'He did not have much opportunity. Soon after they arrived in France he was taken prisoner and later executed in the market place at Lyons. From that time on she had to fend for herself. But that is not necessarily the answer.'

Lucy shook her head. 'There are so many possibilities.'

'Turn the matter over in your mind a few times and you may come to the same conclusion as I have.'

'I wish you would tell me what you mean!'

'All in good time.' The old lady was obviously deriving a certain enjoyment from being mysterious. 'I should prefer you to arrive at the solution by your own route and then we may discover together if we are right. In any event there is no need to hurry.'

Lucy frowned and tried to apply her mind to the problem, but just as she set off along the train of thought suggested by Lady Emilie her attention was diverted by the sight of movement between the trees. 'There's someone coming!' she exclaimed; then, with disappointment, 'I believe it is the Stansgate carriage.'

'Let us pray 'tis not Letty come to pay a duty call,' Lady Emilie remarked with asperity. 'The sight of her frost-bitten countenance depresses me beyond measure these days.'

But when the carriage drew up before the doors of the Dower House they observed two men dismount and enter the house.

'Did you see who it was?' Lady Emilie demanded. 'Is it Ralph at last?'

'I believe so,' said Lucy. 'Do you think he has any news?'

'We shall find out soon enough. No, my dear, there is no need to move. We may as well receive him here, in the garden.'

Indeed, the visitors were already being shown across the lawn. As they drew nearer Lucy stared incredulously at the gaunt figure accompanying Sir Ralph, then started to her feet, sending the novel flying to the ground. 'Papa! Oh, Papa—!'

She hurried towards him, holding out both hands. Never had she been so glad to see her wayward parent, old grievances forgotten as she found herself clasped in an affectionate embrace.

'My dear . . .' Charles Tennant held her at arm's length to study her face. 'Why, you are even paler than I! Not quite as I would wish to see my daughter. But life, I gather, has not been easy for you?'

Lucy shook her head. She gazed up at him, seeing the haggard features and slightly bloodshot eyes that betrayed the effects of his recent ordeal. Yet he had lost none of his old charm as he turned to greet Lady Emilie and assure her of his heartfelt gratitude. The old lady received him stiffly at first, but so contrite was his air and so pleasing his manner that within a few minutes of his arrival she was smiling and tapping him on the arm with her fan in gentle admonishment.

'But, Sir—' Lucy turned in bewilderment to Sir Ralph, who was surveying the tableau with some satisfaction, '—how came my father to be in your company? I understood that—'

'Ah, the actual machinery of your father's release had already been put in motion by my grandmother's man of business in London,' Sir Ralph explained. 'However, since the poor fellow had nowhere to go immediately on the first night of his freedom and was moreover somewhat bemused by the passage of events I sent my carriage to bring him to my London house.'

'Sir Ralph has been most considerate,' said Charles Tennant. 'I was, as he rightly says, completely bewildered by what had happened and he took a great deal of trouble to explain the situation to me.'

'But have you not seen Kitty—or little James?' Lucy inquired.

'Of course. They were in the carriage Sir Ralph sent to meet me. However, on this occasion they have decided to stay in London, though they both send you their warmest love.' His eyes met those of Sir Ralph over her head. 'My visit here is primarily to thank your husband and Lady Emilie for their intervention in my sorry affairs, and secondly to assure myself that you are in good health.'

Lucy looked at him with unhappy eyes. 'My health is good enough, sir, but I fear my spirit is somewhat afflicted.' She turned to Sir Ralph. 'Have you been told what has taken place since you went away?'

'I have heard a garbled version from Letty,' said Sir Ralph, 'and an even more incoherent account from Junot, who came to see me this morning upon my return from London.'

'Then you have been to Brooktye?'

He shook his head. 'I sent Junot back to stay with his master until we were ready to go there ourselves.'

'He will not see anyone.' Lucy's face was white with despair as she turned back to her father. 'Papa, you must by now have realised what a dreadful tangle this is—and how right you were about William.'

'My dear child.' He took hold of both her hands and pressed them reassuringly. 'You must not distress yourself any further. If nothing else I can at least set your mind at rest on that score. You are most certainly *not* married to that young man. Indeed, you never were!'

Lucy stared at him disbelievingly. 'But I don't understand . . . how can you say that? The ceremony was real enough. It was conducted by our own Rector. Are you suggesting that I dreamed it?'

'No, indeed. But I wonder it never occurred to you, my dear, once you realised the man was a trickster of the first order, that you were unlikely to have been his first wife, any more than you were his last. As soon as I recovered from my illness and learned you had been foolish enough to marry him, I had him investigated. To my certain knowledge he was married to one Clara Blackett some two years previously, but when he met you and saw you about to inherit a modest but profitable estate he chose to forget he was already contracted elsewhere. In other words, your marriage was never valid.'

'Not valid?' she echoed.

'When he returned from the Low Countries and discovered I had made such an excellent recovery he realised that the ruse had not succeeded, so he prudently allowed you to think him dead. After that, one presumes, he moved on to pastures new. There is no doubt a score of widows all over the countryside mourning the same gallant soldier. The wars with France must have presented him with endless opportunities for dying on a variety of distant battlefields.'

'Oh, Papa!' Lucy flung herself against his chest. 'Why ever did you not tell me this before?'

'When we received the news of his death it seemed wiser to let well alone. I feared you would be even more shocked to learn how you had been betrayed.'

'We shall find the man, have no fear,' interposed Sir Ralph. 'He shall be brought to justice for what he has done to you—and to Philippe.'

'Philippe!' She raised her head. 'I must go to him now—'

'I agree.' Sir Ralph gave a decisive nod. 'My carriage is at your disposal, Madame.' He glanced at Charles Tennant. 'Will you accompany us, sir?'

'Naturally I should like to meet my son-in-law.'

Lucy looked apprehensive. 'He may refuse to receive us. I do not know if he will even listen to me . . .'

'My dear, nothing we find will shock me, I promise you,' said her father, correctly interpreting her fears. 'I myself am no stranger to despair.'

Sir Ralph turned to his grandmother. 'Will you come with us, Ma'am? Perhaps you are the one person of whom he may take heed.'

Lady Emilie shook her head. 'I think not. But you must go with all speed to tell him the news. It will give him hope for the future.'

'If only I could believe that,' Lucy murmured, her eyes full of unshed tears.

Lady Emilie clasped her in a warm embrace, whispering into her ear, 'You *must* believe it. And when you make your plans, don't forget Junot . . .'

'Of course I shall not forget him.' Lucy drew back to stare into the old lady's face. 'You mean—?'

'Go on, my dear. And hurry!'

As they clattered into the yard at Brooktye Lucy's first thought was that they had come too late. The house looked deserted and wore the same air of neglect and decay as on the first occasion she had set eyes on it.

When Sir Ralph handed her down from the carriage he stared at the charred remains of the barn and the ruined stables. 'Good God!' he muttered under his breath. 'He will never recover from this . . .'

Charles Tennant looked about him without saying a word and put a steadying hand about his daughter's shoulders. At the same moment Junot appeared from what was left of the stables, carrying a broom and in a state of some agitation.

'Oh, Madame! Thank the heavens you have come . . .' He hurried towards her. 'My master—he has great need of you.'

'Junot, how is he? Does he still shut himself away?'

He shook his head. 'Not now the wine has gone. But he is like a dead man . . .'

'Has he asked to see me?' she pleaded.

'No, Madame.' Junot sighed. 'I tell him you are staying with his grandmother but I do not believe he even hears me.'

Charles Tennant squeezed her shoulder. ''Twill be a different matter when he learns of your news,' he whispered encouragingly.

In her heart Lucy doubted if it would make the least difference. By now, she thought, M. de Sevignac was past caring whether or not she were truly his wife. It seemed a matter of small importance compared with the ruin of his vineyard.

'Philippe!' exclaimed Sir Ralph suddenly; and they all turned to follow the direction of his gaze.

M. de Sevignac was standing in the open doorway. The lines of suffering were etched deeply on his face and his eyes, red-rimmed and sunken, regarded them without expression. His apathetic gaze took in Lucy, who stood close to her father, and then his cousin. 'So you have returned, Ralph. Much has happened, as you can see, during your absence.'

Sir Ralph said seriously, 'I am sorry, Philippe. It is indeed a sad sight. However, I bring you some good news at least.' He indicated Charles Tennant. 'This is your father-in-law, released from gaol two days ago, at your instigation.'

The two men looked at each other. Then Charles Tennant said quietly. 'I think M. de Sevignac is not yet ready to receive my thanks. Perhaps we should allow Lucy a little time with him alone so that she may explain the situation.'

'I agree.' Sir Ralph glanced at Lucy. 'We will wait inside the house.'

She was hardly aware of their going. Taking a firm hold of her senses, she began, 'Please, I must speak with you. It is of the utmost importance . . .'

He remained silent, his eyes resting on her dully.

She stepped forward and placed her hand on his arm. He flinched but at least made no effort to evade her grasp. 'Can we not walk a little way?' she said. 'I think I would find it easier to talk . . .'

He allowed her to guide him away from the house, listening without any show of emotion while she told him her news.

When she had finished she stared at him despairingly. 'Does it mean nothing to you, that I am free? Even if you do not love me at least you could let me stay with you. Whatever you decide to do, you need not be alone.' The urge to put her arms around him was strong, but she resisted it, fearing a rebuff. 'Surely you cannot send me away now, after what has happened between us . . . ?'

For a second his eyes blazed, but the light was quickly

extinguished. 'What happened was a mistake. It is best forgotten.'

Hot colour flooded her cheeks. 'You cannot still believe I was merely trying to—to distract your attention from the vineyard? How could I possibly have known what William was planning to do?'

He gave her a sombre look, but made no reply.

'I confess that I—I wanted you to spend the night with me,' she continued recklessly, 'but only because I hoped to make you love me . . .' Her voice tailed away as she gazed up into his bitter, haunted face.

'In that, my dear, I fear you had already succeeded all too well,' he said tonelessly.

Hope sprang alive in her heart. 'Then why must you—?'

'Because it is all over between us. Finished.' He added with cruel emphasis, '*I* am finished. There can be no future for you here, with me.'

'It need not be so!' Desperately she sought for something that would break through his apathy. 'Suppose we have a child—?'

'Then I should of course make some provision for you both.'

'Oh, Philippe—why can you not accept that I love you?' She saw him wince and pressed on, fearful that this might be her last chance to convince him she spoke the truth. 'I cannot bear your indifference. Be angry, if you will—*hate* me, even . . . but for pity's sake let me stay!'

He gazed at her wonderingly; then, in a voice still roughened by the after-effects of smoke and the wine he had consumed, he said 'It is kind of you to offer, Madame, but I can promise you nothing but poverty now. It is better we should part—'

'What do I care for poverty? I would gladly live with you in the merest hovel, if we must.'

'I believe you mean it,' he said, sounding surprised.

'However, I have no intention of inflicting such a life upon you. Now that your father is free you have a family to turn to once again.'

She stood still and declared firmly, 'I should not dream of returning to live with them. I am a married woman. My place is with my husband.'

But already his eyes had wandered away from her. With a shock she realised they were standing beside the empty, desecrated vineyard. Suddenly she was seized by a burst of impatient anger. Could nothing she say make any impression on him?

'We can plant more vines,' she continued in desperation. 'You have done it before—you can do it again. Or return to France—'

He turned and began to walk away from her.

'Philippe, listen to me!' She ran after him. 'I know you attribute my interest in the jewels to the basest motives, but your grandmother and I have been giving some thought to the matter and we believe we know where they may be found.'

He gave no sign that he had heard her, making his way back to the yard. Junot appeared at once from the stables, still carrying his broom.

'Go take some refreshment to my cousin and Madame's father,' his master ordered. 'Tell them I apologise for my discourtesy and will join them as soon as I have washed the dirt from my hands.'

'No, Junot—wait,' Lucy interrupted, breathless from hurrying.

He turned to her inquiringly. 'Yes, Madame?'

She took a deep breath. 'Do you wish to return to France?'

'With all my heart!' The words burst from him impulsively, but as soon as they were out he looked with contrition at his master. 'I am sorry, Monsieur. Naturally I go wherever you go.'

Lucy said, 'He would return to France, Junot, if he had enough money to buy back his land.'

He turned to M. de Sevignac. 'Is that true, Monsieur?'

His master shrugged. 'What is the point of torturing ourselves by dreaming of what we cannot have?'

Lucy went on, 'So you see, Junot, the time has come for you to give back the jewels you have been hiding ever since the night that Madame—the first Madame de Sevignac—left for France. The jewels you exchanged for stones . . .'

Junot stared at her open-mouthed.

'You can rest assured,' she continued, 'they will not be squandered, as you feared, but will instead be put to the use you always intended for them. To restore the old vineyards . . .'

He glanced quickly at his master. 'Monsieur, this is so?'

After a long pause M. de Sevignac said, 'Certainly it is so. If the inheritance is still in our possession what else should we do but sell it—and return to France?'

'Wait here. I will fetch the jewels.' Swinging round on his heel, Junot set off at a trot towards the house.

M. de Sevignac turned slowly to his wife. 'Can this be true? But how on earth—?'

'It was your grandmother.' Lucy's eyes were brilliant. 'She reasoned that it had to be someone else, someone who was also in the house that night. It could only have been Armand . . . or Junot. And Armand would hardly have tricked his own sister.'

'But why should Junot—?'

'He regards himself as your guardian angel. He knew that if you had the jewels you would eventually be tempted to spend the money on the vineyard here at Brooktye, but his dearest wish was to return to France. So when the jewels came into his hands he decided to keep them hidden until such time as it would be possible to go back. Only, being Junot, he was not always as discreet as he might have been, especially when he had been drinking at the Talbot. That is how the rumours spread of a treasure hidden in the house—the rumours that William heard.'

M. de Sevignac shook his head. 'I shall not believe it until I see them. Where could he have hidden them?'

'Heaven alone knows!' Lucy smiled at him, her face glowing. ''Tis a wonder William did not find them when he was searching the house. If I had known they were there I certainly would not have suggested he make such a thorough search.'

'I fear I have wronged you dreadfully,' he said in a serious tone.

'Oh, Philippe . . .' She stepped closer to him, holding out her hands. 'Tell me honestly, are you not beginning to feel more hopeful about our future at last?'

He took her hands and lifted them to his lips. 'My nature is to be cautious, as you know, but I will admit to just a hint of optimism.' He gazed down at her. 'It is all very well for Junot and I to talk of returning to France, but what of you? Could you be happy in another country, or would it not then be *you* who is in exile?'

She smiled. 'Woman build their lives around the people they love, not places. Anywhere away from you would be exile.'

He drew her gently towards him. 'Oh, my dearest love . . .'

Before their lips could meet Junot burst from the house carrying a small portmanteau. 'Here they are, Monsieur! I have them safe . . .' Panting, he held the bag towards his master like a dog who has just retrieved a stick.

M. de Sevignac opened the bag an inch or two and said. '*Mon Dieu!*'

'They have grown dull,' Junot said anxiously, 'but will

soon come clean.' To prove his words he pulled out an emerald clasp and rubbed it on his sleeve.

Speechless, M. de Sevignac shook his head and for the first time a smile of genuine amusement transformed his face.

'Junot, you are wonderful!' Lucy hugged him joyfully.

He beamed. 'I have done a good thing, yes? Monsieur and Madame are pleased with me?'

'One of these days I shall tell you what I really think of you,' said M. de Sevignac, 'but at the moment I seem unable to find adequate words!'

When all the talking was done and M. de Sevignac had made his father-in-law's acquaintance and received his thanks, the visitors departed from Stansgate Hall, where Charles Tennant was to spend the night at Sir Ralph's invitation before returning on the morrow to his wife and son in London.

'You know, there are times when I am almost fond of Ralph,' M. de Sevignac remarked to his wife as they watched the carriage depart. 'He's a philanderer, 'tis true, though I think he was not altogether to blame for what happened with Madeleine, since the fault was partly hers. But at least he has a heart, which is rather more than one can say for poor Letty.'

Lucy nodded her agreement. 'Papa has his faults as well, but I cannot help loving him all the same.' She gave him a mischievous smile. 'Though I am glad I do not have to live with him and Kitty after all!'

M. de Sevignac looked shocked. 'The very idea! A woman's place is with her husband, as you have already observed. Though heaven only knows where your husband's place may be!'

By mutual consent they began to walk up the path towards the vineyard, their arms about each other. 'I wonder if Ralph will ever manage to find William,' Lucy mused. 'He seems determined to do so.'

'I must admit I do not greatly care. What is done is done and I'd as soon forget about it. Mollie Thrupp has disappeared, by the way. It may be she has gone to join him.'

'Strangely enough, I believe she loves him, despite the way he treats her.' Lucy shuddered.

He smiled. 'Women are such strange creatures.' He pulled her against him so that she stood within the circle of his arm. Together they surveyed the blackened remains of the vineyard. 'There is at least one thing in all this that pleases me,' he said at length. 'I have proved it can be done. Grapes *will* grow in this unpredictable climate. England *could* produce her own wine, if she put her mind to it.'

Lucy smiled up at him. 'Yes, it can be done. But not, I think, by us.'

'No, not by us,' he agreed, without regret. He glanced down at her. 'You are—quite sure?'

'Quite sure.' She gave a sigh of deep content.

He said gravely, 'I love you, Lucy. I believe I have loved you since that first day when you walked into the drawing-room and looked through the window at the vines. I wanted to tell you so before but I could not. Now—'

'I know.' She put her fingers over his mouth. 'Now 'tis different. You've come back to life again. And we can plan for the future . . .'

He kissed her fingers and then took away her hand so that he might cover her mouth with his. They clung together, rapturously oblivious to the presence of their guardian angel, who was observing the scene with a satisfied smile upon his good-natured face.

Romance for Mother's Day

You love Mills &
Boon romances.
So will your mother.
The Mills & Boon
Mother's Day Gift
Pack is published
on February 11th
in the UK.
It contains four new
Mills & Boon paper-
back romances, in
a most attractive
presentation case:

Distrust her Shadow	— Jessica Steel
Man with Two Faces	— Jane Corrie
One Man Woman	— Jessica Ayre
My Lord Kasseem	— Mons Daveson

It's on sale where you buy paperbacks. £3.80 (UK net)

Mills & Boon
The rose of romance

How to join in a whole new world of romance

It's very easy to subscribe to the Mills & Boon Reader Service. As a regular reader, you can enjoy a whole range of special benefits. Bargain offers. Big cash savings. Your own free Reader Service newsletter, packed with knitting patterns, recipes, competitions, and exclusive book offers.

We send you the very latest titles each month, postage and packing free – no hidden extra charges. There's absolutely no commitment – you receive books for only as long as you want.

We'll send you details. Simply send the coupon – or drop us a line for details about the Mills & Boon Reader Service Subscription Scheme. Post to: Mills & Boon Reader Service, P.O. Box 236, Thornton Road, Croydon, Surrey CR9 3RU, England. *Please note: READERS IN SOUTH AFRICA please write to: Mills & Boon Ltd., P.O. Box 1872, Johannesburg 2000, S. Africa.

Please send me details of the Mills & Boon Subscription Scheme.

NAME (Mrs/Miss) _____ EP3

ADDRESS _____

_____

COUNTY/COUNTRY_____ POST/ZIP CODE_____

BLOCK LETTERS, PLEASE

Mills & Boon

the rose of romance